CATCH ME

Shade Owens

www.shadeowens.com

Edited by Nikki Busch
www.nikkibuschediting.com

RED RAVEN PUBLISHING

ISBN: 978-1-990271-20-5

Prologue

I could drink myself into a stupor (and trust me, I've tried), or pop as many pills as humanly possible, but I know that no matter how much effort I put into obliterating her from my memory, I will never forget the first time I saw her.

It was a cold, mid-September, Friday afternoon—a boring school day like any other. I was zoning out at the back of Mr. Tanore's English class, when ten minutes to the bell she walked in accompanied by our principal. She had long, silky black hair and the brightest green eyes I'd ever seen. Mr. Tanore froze mid-sentence and a few words were whispered between him and the principal.

"Everyone, I'd like you all to welcome our newest student, Samantha Boward," Mr. Tanore finally announced.

His crooked, gray mustache twitched at one

end as it always did when he was feeling uneasy. No one spoke, and Samantha didn't smile. Her eyes carelessly scanned the room.

"Hi, Sam!" Jack called out.

Jack Durham—the loud, goofy moron—somehow managed to make people laugh, regardless of how immature his comments tended to be. Samantha didn't reply. She stared. I could tell this wasn't going to be an easy change.

Mr. Tanore cleared his throat and extended an arm in my direction. "Well, Samantha, you can have a seat beside Kaitlyn, and we'll continue on with the lesson."

That's when my chest tightened. Her cold stare suddenly turned on me, and she started walking my way. I felt butterflies drowning in the pit of my stomach, and my hands became clammy. She was so beautiful, yet so terrifying with her crystal-green eyes outlined in black. Who stares that long? I felt my face turn bright red, so I turned away. I couldn't quite pinpoint the source of my fear, nor could I determine whether or not I was enjoying it as one does a scary movie.

She sat down, dropped her black, safety-pinned bag by her chair with a thud, pulled out a pencil and a sheet of paper, and raised one of her legs onto the desk's metal side bar. I looked down at her studded black leather boots and then up at her. It felt as though someone had punched me in the gut when she caught me staring.

"What the fuck are you looking at?" she asked.

And at that moment, I knew that although everything about her warned all living beings to keep their distance, I did somehow, perhaps masochistically, enjoy her presence.

Chapter 1

As I made my way to the school bus that afternoon, thinking about how unprepared I was to see her again, I heard her raspy voice call out, "Hey, you."

I considered ignoring her altogether. There were hundreds of students out there in search of their own buses; why would she be calling out to me? But, feeling somewhat rude and also curious, I turned around. There she was—an unlit smoke in one hand and the "no-smoking" sign wrapped underneath the fingers of her other hand. I stared, speechless. She was definitely looking at me. What did she want? I noticed a smirk curve the corner of her lips, and she swung her head to the side, signaling me to approach. So, I did.

"Got a light?" she asked.

"No, sorry." I said it much more quickly than I had planned.

I became uncomfortable when I noticed she was still staring at me, so I smiled and turned around before she could notice I was blushing.

"Hey, wait," she said.

What now? I wanted to run to my bus, to pretend that Samantha didn't exist. How could such a person make another so nervous? I didn't get it. I turned back to face her, and again, forced a halfhearted smile.

"Who are they?" she asked me.

"Who?" I asked, following her bright eyes.

They led me to a group of three girls who were giggling.

"The ones pointing and laughing. Kinda hard to miss, don't you think?" she asked.

And sure enough, the three girls were standing at the end of the school's parking lot, pointing in my direction and laughing among themselves. Although they were strangers to Samantha, they were no strangers to me.

I laughed uncomfortably, but she didn't find it amusing. Her eyes narrowed on me, and she tilted her head.

"Are they laughing at you or at me?" she asked.

I weakened. Her eyes were deadly. But the good news was that I knew precisely what those girls were laughing about—they did it nearly every day when I walked past them: "Lesbo," "Dyke," or "Rug-Muncher," were their usual shouts. Why? Because they thought I was gay. Because I wasn't like the other girls. I had never been. I wasn't overly feminine, and I had no interest in boys.

"Oh, um, me," I said.

"You sure?" she asked, now glaring at them.

I knew this had saved me. They weren't laughing at her; therefore, she had no reason to be upset.

"I'm sure." I smiled. She didn't reply, so I nodded and started walking away.

"I'm not done," she said.

Kill me now, I thought.

Once again, I retraced my steps and found myself facing Samantha. I raised my eyebrows and waited.

"What are they laughing at, exactly?" she asked.

What did she care? She barely knew me. I didn't understand how this was any of her business, and quite honestly, I thought it was a little intrusive of her to ask. My thoughts must have found their way to my face; she grinned—the most stunning grin, I might add—and shook her head.

"Oh don't get all offended. It's just a question," she said. "Oh, hey, got a light?"

Did she suffer from memory loss? I gawked at her.

"I already told you, I don't—" I said, but then

some guy behind me reached out a lighter and lit her cigarette. I felt like an idiot.

"Thanks, man," she said. She blew her smoke out in my direction and smiled again.

"Well?"

"Well, what?" I asked.

"What. Are. They..." she said, emphasizing each word.

Now she was just being rude.

"They call me a lesbian," I said.

"Are you?" she asked. Wow, again with the intrusiveness.

"No," I blurted out quickly.

I wanted to return her the question, but even I knew that it wasn't very polite, not that Samantha had any knowledge of the term politeness. Besides, what did I care if she was gay or not?

"Even if you were gay, I don't see how that'd be worth a laugh." She blew out another lungful of smoke and reached down to grab her bag. "See you around Kaitlyn." She started walking towards the lesbian-trashing group.

Oh no. What was she going to do? Fight them? It would be three against one; although they were rather tiny girls, Samantha would probably win. No, she wouldn't start a fight over me, would she? I stared wide-eyed, afraid of what was about to come. From this distance, I noticed the group of girls tense at the sight of

Samantha's angered arrival. They grabbed their bags and ran to their bus, quickly boarding it.

Samantha's long, black jacket swam through the wind in perfect alignment with the waves of her hair as she moved straight forward. There was no turning to even look at the girls, no attempt to chase them—nothing. She walked along, passing all of the buses, and continued down the street and onto a small path leading into the forest. I sighed in relief.

I went home with a feeling of exhilaration I couldn't explain. I had never felt this before. Fear? Happiness? Worry? A crush? How could I have a crush on a girl? I wasn't gay. I couldn't be. I had just broken up with my boyfriend. Although, I did have a tendency to get nervous around pretty girls, and I'd never had sex with a boy because I thought it repulsive. Shit, maybe I was a lesbian. No. I wasn't. I mean, the thought had crossed my mind before even meeting Samantha, but I had pushed it away. I couldn't be. I couldn't. But maybe...

BEED-A-LEEP.

I reached into my pocket and pulled out my cell. A text from Matt. Matthew Semmer. Speak of the devil. My ex-boyfriend. It read,

"Can I plz c u tonight?"

I didn't hesitate. I typed in a clear "NO," still fed by my anger at his overly persistent attempts at getting sex from me. But, right before I pressed send, I realized something. It was Friday night, and I had no plans. I wasn't in the mood to be alone, nor did I want to stay in. I backspaced my reply and replaced it with:

"Only if there's a party going on."

Hah. That was perfect. He'd get drunk, as he always did, and I could go off to do my own thing, as I always did. I threw off my shoes and ran upstairs to my small, cozy room. I plopped down on my bed and stared at my ceiling. It was a very white, very plain ceiling. And that's when I realized that the only decorations visible in my room were karate trophies and yellow happy-face stickers. Where were the boys? My sister's room had tons of hunks smiling down at her.

Why was I suddenly questioning my sexuality? Because Samantha accepted it? What did I care what Samantha thought? I knew nothing about her. But for the hell of it, I imagined what it would be like to have a very attractive woman smiling down at me, sporting nothing but a thin, red bikini. To be honest, it did nothing but make me uncomfortable. So I blinked those thoughts away and attempted to visualize a man—a tanned hunk with a muscular six-pack. Nothing. If anything, I was jealous of his abs. What the hell was going on? I took a deep breath and closed my eyes.

BEED-A-LEEP.

Yes! A distraction! From Matt,

"Ya, there's a party. Wanna go? Kim's place."

Kimberly Tompson. Yeah, you guessed it. One of the populars. But hey, stereotypes aren't always accurate. Kim was rather nice and pleasant to be around. She wasn't insecure, and therefore, had no reason to mock the smaller people. She spoke to me when she needed help with a mathematical equation or when she apologized on behalf of her half-brained friends. I always turned tomato red every time she leaned in close. I remember having stuttered out a wordless answer when her breast had accidentally pressed up against my shoulder. With all of these clues, I was beginning to solve a rainbow puzzle.

I shook out of my daze and replied to Matt's text:

"Sounds good. What time?"

I had barely put down my phone when it went off again. Wow, someone was excited.

"Great! 9. I'll pick u up then."

I was about to reply, *I can get there myself,* but realized this was a little harsh. It was better to have a friend than an enemy. After all, he was just a horny boy. It wasn't his fault he wanted to sleep with me so badly. I figured it was best to accept this as a compliment, rather than as an offensive gesture. But then again, he should have respected my wishes. I have rights too. Oh man, was I now a feminist? Enough thinking for one night! I needed rest if I was going to make it past nine. Very old woman of me, I know.

So I closed my eyes and turned onto my side. And although I had no intention of shifting my thoughts in such a direction, I suddenly realized that I was visualizing Samantha's perfect white face.

* * *

KNOCK, KNOCK.

"Kaity, supper's ready." My mom's voice penetrated my sleep.

I opened my tired eyes and looked around, completely disoriented. The party! That's right.

"Coming," I moaned.

It was the same routine every night: my mother, my father, my older sister Amy, and I gathered at the dining room table for supper. You could say we were your typical *perfect family*. As I made my way down the stairs, the savory smell of seasoned chicken breast filled my nostrils. Amy was already out of her room and opening a bottle of white wine for my parents and herself. I filled my plate with food and sat down.

"So, any plans for tonight?" my mother asked, eyeing both my sister and me from behind her stiff, red bangs.

Amy spoke first. "Actually, I have a date." The smile on her face nearly reached her ears.

My mother grabbed her hand and grinned. They looked like sisters. Fire twins. I sometimes wondered whether or not I had been adopted. They were both pale, petite in size, red-haired, and green-eyed. My father's hair was dark brown like mine, but our personalities were nothing alike. He was too stern. I had to have been adopted, I thought, staring at the *two sisters* and wondering if I'd ever been that excited about anything in my life before.

"Really?" my mother asked. "What's his name? What does he look like? What does he do?"

"No sex in this house," my father intervened, pointing his fork at Amy.

"Dad!" Amy shouted, her nose wrinkled with disgust. "His name's Andrew. He's so handsome. I met him in my psych class today. I still can't get over how many hot guys go to uni."

"Amy and Andrew," I chuckled. "Cute."

"Shut up," she said, laughing.

"All right, well that's great!" my mother said. "Is he picking you up?"

"Yep," Amy said, smirking. "He drives a Lancer."

My mother's eyes widened, but my father spoke first. "Good, because he's coming in here to meet us."

"Dad!" Amy whined.

"Your father's right. I want to meet this

hunk of yours," my mom said, winking terribly with her mouth half-open.

The embarrassing sister, I thought.

All of this date talk led them to forget about me. But I didn't care. I was used to receiving minimal attention. We finished supper and the clock turned to seven pretty fast. Amy was all dressed, her hair and makeup touched up to perfection. I thought it cute how my mother had also brushed on a little powder for presentation. At precisely 7:02, the bell rang. I poked my head out from the staircase to observe. I wanted to see what this *gorgeous fella* looked like.

Right as he walked in, I understood why Amy liked him. He had a prominent jaw structure; clean, blond hair; and bright blue eyes. Your average Ken, I thought, snickering to myself. A grown man. Nothing like Matt, who was tall and scrawny. Not that there's anything wrong with being a thin guy, but in Matt's case, his size easily shaved five years off his appearance, which wasn't necessarily a positive thing for an eighteen-year-old guy.

The meeting of parents seemed to have gone smoothly; my dad shook Andrew's hand and patted him on the back.

"You take good care of her for us, all right?" my dad said.

"Absolutely, sir," Andrew said, and he led

Amy out of the house with such tenderness, that I wondered whether or not he'd have the muscles ready to catch her if she happened to slip.

The car pulled out within minutes, and it was now my turn to get ready. Unlike Amy, I simply threw on a pair of nice, tight jeans, and a black T-shirt. Simplicity was key. Why bother getting all dressed up to be uncomfortable? I wasn't going out to meet anyone; what did I care? At a quarter to nine, I went back downstairs and realized my parents were already getting ready for bed.

"Where do you think you're going?" my father asked.

"Oh, I'm going to a party with Matt."

"Matt? That boy you broke up with?" my mom asked, joining in on the interrogation.

"Yup."

They both exchanged confused glances, but then shrugged and smiled.

"All right, well, no drinking, no smoking, and be back by ten," my father ordered.

"Ten? Dad! The party starts at nine, come on," I said.

Yeah, I know what you're thinking—he must have been joking. I would have assumed the same thing from a third-party point of view, but my father wasn't the type to deliver funnies.

"Come on Jon, don't be such a downer," my mom said. "Kaity, as long as you come back home, you can stay out as late as you want."

"Thanks, Mom." I hugged them both and made my way to the kitchen for a quick cookie feast.

I could hear some bickering behind me. I hoped I wouldn't be the cause of a marital fight.

BEED-A-LEEP.

I opened my phone. Matt:

"I'm outside."

I said my goodbyes, and I was out of there.

Kim's house was at the opposite end of the city, a good fifteen minutes away. I noticed Matt stir in his seat a bit, and I knew precisely what was about to unfold—a relationship talk. So, I blasted the music and smiled at him. His attempt ended before it had even begun.

We parked on the street since the driveway was already packed. I'd been there once before, the previous year. The house was extremely spacious and perfect for parties, unlike my parents' place, which contained too many glass vases and delicate decorations. Kim's parents were always out of town for business, which proved to be quite convenient for her social life.

A dozen empty cases of different types of beer were piled up in the oversized foyer, just as they had been last time. The full cases were probably already loaded in the fridge. I slid off my shoes and entered. Everything was loud—the music, the chatting, the clinking of glasses and beer bottles. Not even five minutes into the party, Matt had abandoned me to go drink with his buddies. I knew I'd be driving his drunk ass home, which was fine by me, so long as he didn't try anything stupid.

"Hey Kaity!" came a familiar voice.

I turned and spotted Jody Smith, a girl from my English class—one of the only familiar faces there. I assumed that everyone from school would be here, but I was mistaken. Kim's main followers were here of course, but the party consisted mostly of brand new faces.

"Hey, what are you doing here? I didn't know you were friends with Kim," I said.

"Nah, I'm here with Chris. I'm not sure where he's at right now," she said.

Her boyfriend, I assumed. I didn't know all that much about her.

"Ah, I see. He's probably getting sloshed with Matt." I forced an awkward laugh.

"You guys are back together?"

"Oh, um. No, not really. We're friends now," I said.

I wondered how we'd ever started dating. I was never attracted to him; I didn't even like him romantically.

She smiled and raised her plastic cup.

"Want a drink?" she asked.

"No, I'm good, thanks."

I didn't drink. I had never had a drink in my life. What was the point? I looked around for reassurance, and sure enough, it was received—people stumbling, others slurring their sentences, most guys groping the girls they desired most. Disgusting, really. Animalistic behavior.

"All right, well, I'm in the living room with my friends if you want to join us," she said.

I couldn't refuse. I had nowhere else to go, so I followed her. As she started introductions, I spotted long, shiny, black hair. My heart sank and I swallowed hard. Samantha? Samantha was already friends with Jody and not with me? What the hell was she doing here? I could feel my hands getting clammy as they always did. I tried hard to focus on the people being introduced to me, but their names went right over my head. I smiled, staring blankly at them. I shook a few hands before I was finally about to be introduced to Samantha.

"Shay, meet Kaitlyn," Jody said.

The black-haired girl turned to face me. She had large brown eyes and a silly grin on her face. My heart regained its regular beat. Of course it wasn't Samantha. What had I been thinking? Samantha? Bitchy girl. Coming to Kim's party? I extended my hand and smiled.

What a scare, I thought. Although I was somewhat relieved, I also wished it had been Samantha.

The party consisted mainly of Cheetos, water, and bathroom breaks for me, as I watched everyone else fall to pieces. When the clock reached two a.m., Matt came stumbling around a corner in search of me.

"Kaity!" he shouted, sprinkling saliva on my face.

"I'm right here," I said, my voice dull. I wiped the underneath of my right eye.

"There you arrrre, sexy!" he said.

Oh, great. He was going to be a handful. I only hoped the music would silence him again during the ride home.

"You ready to go?" I asked.

"Only if you are," he said, nearly losing his balance.

One eye was noticeably smaller than the other (the eyes of a drunk), but I didn't find it humorous. It was pathetic, really.

"Come on." I grabbed his arm tightly, led him to his car, and pushed him into the passenger seat. He willingly gave me his keys and smiled.

"Where we going?" he asked, excitement in his drunken voice.

"You're going home, and so am I."

"Oh realllyyy?" he said.

"You're going to your home, and I'm going to mine," I clarified.

"You know, Kaity—" he said.

And I blasted the music before shifting out of park and speeding away from Kim's house.

I drove as fast as legally acceptable, not wanting him to speak to me. But when I looked over, he'd fallen asleep. Well, passed out. I pulled into his driveway and slammed the breaks to wake him. His head rocked forward and he mumbled something incomprehensible, opened his eyes, and stared at me.

"Where are we?" he asked.

"You're home. Get out, please. You can come get your car tomorrow, okay? Have a good night, Matt."

I was tired and getting moody. I didn't have time to babysit. What's worse was that regardless of my unfriendliness, he still leaned in for a kiss. I nearly laughed in his face, but regained my composure and pushed him away.

"Matt, I'm not your girlfriend. We're friends now. Friends don't kiss."

"Friends with benefits do," he said, sliding a suggestive hand down my thigh.

"Alright, perv. Go drink some water. I'll talk to you tomorrow."

Like a gentleman, I hopped out of my seat, walked around the car, and opened his door to help him out.

"Come on. Let's go," I said.

He did as he was told and stumbled to the front of his house. I jumped back into the driver's seat and watched him struggle to unlock the front door. I shook my head and laughed. I kind of felt sorry for him. But that feeling didn't last very long. I pulled out and drove away, eagerly wanting to jump into my warm, cozy bed and sleep my weekend away. All I wanted at this point was for Monday to come around. Samantha would be there.

Chapter 2

Although I didn't sleep the weekend away, it did pass by quickly. A lot of movies and junk food aided me in my quest. I prepared my school lunch Monday morning and ran to the bus stop when it was time to leave.

I was anxious the entire ride to school. Why? Because of Samantha. I felt so dumb. When I finally arrived, my eyes didn't rest. I continuously scanned my surroundings. I was nervous, but I wanted to see her. Only one look. I wanted her to see me. As irrational as I was being, I couldn't help my wanting.

My first class was Science. Was she going to be in it? I crossed my fingers and entered the classroom. To my disappointment, Samantha wasn't there. The anxiety followed me to Math and then to History; it left me, only to be replaced with disappointment. Finally, English. Surely, she would be present beside me.

Wouldn't she? She had attended English class last Friday.

An alien sadness overwhelmed me when I realized that her seat was empty. My papers were now pointlessly damp due to anxiety, and Samantha was nowhere to be seen. I sighed and went on with my day.

Supper went the same as usual that night— Amy went on about how wonderful Andrew was and how she wished she'd met him sooner. I didn't have much to say; I preferred to listen. That is, when I wasn't daydreaming about Samantha. How could a person have such a strong hold on me? I was losing my mind. Perhaps if I spoke to her, these mysterious feelings would go away. It was only a matter of facing my fear.

Tuesday came around, and Samantha was still not there. Maybe she'd decided to change schools after Friday afternoon? Perhaps something had happened that I was unaware of. I counted the days painfully, hoping every morning that I would see her. When Thursday came around, I was doodling some crap in my Math binder when I realized that it was probably best to forget about her. She wasn't coming back.

"Sorry I'm late," came a cold voice.

It didn't quite click at first, but when my eyes rolled up to the front of the class, I saw her. She wore baggy brown pants and a tight, white T-shirt. What a perfect body, I thought. Our eyes locked and she walked my way. Samantha, in my Math class?

"Could you please move? You're in my seat," Samantha said, staring down at Jessica Law, some girl who sat beside me.

"But this is—" Jessica said.

"Look, I don't want any trouble," Samantha said, an exaggerated smile plastered on her face.

Jessica looked for the teacher's eyes, but they were facing the chalkboard. Samantha leaned over, placed an elbow on Jessica's desk, and narrowed her eyes.

"I'm going to give you three seconds," she said.

I wanted to scream. Scream with joy. I wanted to hug Samantha but run at the same time. She wanted to sit beside me. Me! Out of all people. Did I have this same hold on her, too? I hoped so.

Jessica stumbled out of her seat, binder in hand, and made her way to an empty desk at the back of the classroom. There were whispers shared among the students, but no one spoke up. Mrs. Demmy was still chalking away, completely oblivious to the entire spectacle.

"Oh, you again," Samantha said, glancing sideways at me.

You again? She had picked that seat! Had she truly not seen me, or was she simply playing mind games? I smiled as best as I could and looked away. Although uncertain of her true thoughts, I could have sworn I heard her exhale a laugh.

We didn't speak again that day. She was quiet in English class, and I saw her walk home alone, as she'd done the previous Friday. So she lived near the school, I concluded. This made me feel slightly stalkerish, so I hopped on the bus and blasted my iPod.

I rested my head against the bus window, completely out of touch with reality. I replayed those three words she had said, *Oh, you again.* Did she not like me? Or maybe she did, which was why she had sat down right next to me. *Please like me*, I thought. I suddenly visualized Samantha's lips pressed against mine, and an electric jolt shot from my neck down to my pelvic area.

"Kaity!"

I snapped out of it, slightly ashamed of what I had felt. It was Jody, the one from the party. I didn't know she took this school bus.

"Hey, Jody," I said.

"I'm not following you," she said laughing. "I recently moved to the East End, so I'm on your bus now." She hopped in the seat next to mine and grinned.

"Oh, no way! Very cool," I said.

We chatted about all sorts of things: boys, mainly. But all I could think about was Samantha.

"Well, this is my stop! See you tomorrow," Jody said as she rose to exit the bus.

When I walked through the door of my house, Amy came running down the stairs, a huge childlike grin causing her cheeks to balloon.

"Kaity! Get dressed. We're going out for supper," she said.

"Why?" I asked, nonchalantly.

"Why not? Andrew's joining us. A nice family supper for you guys to get to know him." She bounced up and down and ran back upstairs.

Great. Well, I hadn't gone out to eat in a very long time, so I supposed it would be nice. I was all dressed up—tight black dress pants and a silky purple top—by the time my parents came home.

"Oh, Kaity, don't you have a dress or something?" my mother asked.

What was so fascinating about dresses? It was the same story every time. I didn't like dresses, okay? I pulled my long, straight brown hair back into a ponytail and gawked at her.

"Mom, I look fine like this."

"All right, all right. I only wish you'd be more ladylike sometimes," she said.

I rolled my eyes and walked away. At the same time, Amy came rushing down in a red dress, a pair of red heels held tightly in the elbow of her arm.

"Mom, tie me up, please!" she urged and turned around.

My mother zipped her up, turned her around, and grabbed her shoulders.

"You look incredible," she said. "You must have guys lined up for you in class."

Amy laughed and fixed her lipstick in the mirror. I stared at them for a moment and went off to eat a cookie. *You look incredible* I repeated in my head. Blah blah blah blah blah. I looked good too, but instead, I constantly received tips on how I could look better. I didn't want to be better. I wanted to be me.

"We're leaving in ten!" my mother announced.

"Patricia, how do I look?" My father came down the stairs with open palms.

My mom's jaw dropped, and she grinned up at the handsome, well-dressed man heading in her direction. She grabbed his face and kissed him on the lips. He did look good—a black suit, a white button-down shirt, a black tie, and shiny black shoes. His dark hair was gelled back—he looked like James Bond!

As you have probably already guessed, our family didn't go out very often. So when we did, it was an event. At precisely six o'clock, the bell rang. Punctual—impressive, I thought. Andrew was welcomed with open arms and we hopped into my parents' silver Santa Fe. The restaurant, The Blue Crystal, was located in the heart of downtown Loshano. It was pretty busy when we arrived, but my mother had of course made reservations.

As we looked over the menu, I learned that Andrew was aiming to become an electrical engineer. He currently worked with his dad as a mechanic, and he was religious—a perfect match for my parents. Oh, and for Amy. A lot more information had been shared, but I zoned out halfway through the conversation.

"Kaity?" my mother asked.

"Huh?" I mumbled.

I suddenly realized that I had been staring at my waitress's short-skirted legs.

"Are you ready to order?" she asked, looking at me and then at the waitress.

The young, blonde-haired woman stared at me, pen and pad in hand. How embarrassing. Had she caught me staring?

"Uhm... I'll have a burger and fries, please," I said quickly.

I saw Amy wrinkle her nose.

"She's only joking," she assured our waitress, "she wants number ten, please, with a side of steamed vegetables."

I had no idea what number ten was, but I smiled and nodded when the waitress looked at me. I tried to read the menu to see what had been ordered for me, but the waitress had been too quick. She snatched up the menus, smiled politely, and assured us that it wouldn't be too long.

I didn't bother asking Amy what she'd gotten me. I figured I had already embarrassed her enough in front of Andrew. Our meals finally arrived, and to be honest, I had wanted to comment on the portion size, but refrained from doing so. Before my eyes—which were probably larger than the meal itself at that moment—was a ridiculously small salmon fillet sautéed in butter, with a very tiny serving of steamed vegetables at its side.

It was tasty, but I didn't care about that when the bill showed up. I popped my head beside my dad (something classy, well-educated people don't do, apparently) and read the total: $396.25. What. The. Fuck. I could have purchased three microwaves and a year's supply of Kraft Dinner with that money! Or better yet, a 120 GB Play Station 3! Gah!

"That's almost four hundred dollars!" I shouted.

I hadn't realized how loud my words were. I saw Amy's face turn red when a few tables turned their heads in our direction. The waitress leaned in and asked, "Is there a problem here?"

"No problem," my father said, smiling and raising an open palm.

He pulled out his Visa card and handed it to the waitress. No one spoke, but their eyes told me everything. I decided it best to shut my mouth for the remainder of the evening. To avoid being yelled at or given a lecture, I ran to my room when we arrived home and jumped into bed. I wasn't in the mood to be talked down to. I was always doing something wrong.

I didn't even bother to brush my teeth or wash my face. Instead, I locked my door and went to sleep on a full stomach, which made falling asleep that much easier. But I knew I could only evade the consequences of my actions for so long when I woke up the next morning. I went downstairs after my shower and, as expected, my mother was standing in the kitchen.

"Kaity, about last night—" she said.

"Look, I know I was an idiot. And I'm sorry. I've never been to a high-class restaurant before, but I promise to keep my mouth shut next time," I said, before allowing her the opportunity to bash me.

To my surprise, she didn't reply. Instead, she nodded and left the room. I got ready for school, as I did every day, and made my way to the bus stop. Did I belong in my family? I felt like an alien... like the black sheep. I blasted my iPod to escape my reality and stepped onto the bus.

Jody was there, waving at me. Irritated at the thought of having to socialize, I forced a smile, removed my earbuds, and sat down beside her.

I told her about my restaurant incident, which somehow turned out to be a relief. She laughed at the idea of any restaurant charging so much and told me that she'd have done the same thing in my shoes. Maybe Jody wasn't so bad after all. It was me—I wasn't very social.

I walked into Math class and looked up at the board: "Assignments on my desk, please."

Shit! I had completely forgotten. I slid a hand through my hair and sighed.

"Want the answers?" I heard someone ask.

I turned to my left and spotted Samantha. Samantha! How had I forgotten about her? How had I not seen her? I looked down on her desk and saw that she had completed the assignment. But I wasn't a cheater. I couldn't. I wouldn't.

I opened my mouth, but nothing came out.

"What's wrong?" she asked. She tilted her head to the side, a sly smirk on her lips. "Are you scared of me?"

I couldn't answer.

"Do I make you nervous?" she said, that evil smile still on her face.

"No," I finally said.

"No, what?"

"I'm not scared of you," I lied. And I also avoided commenting on how nervous she made me. I didn't look at her to see her reaction.

Fortunately, Mrs. Demmy suddenly spoke up, "Those of you who didn't complete the assignment, grab your desk and go finish it in the hallway."

Great. How embarrassing. I sighed, stood up, and screeched my desk towards the door. I heard a few people laugh, but the ruckus ended abruptly when I noticed Samantha got up and did the same. What was she doing? She had finished her assignment! My heart raced. This was it. She was going to torture me to put me in my place. Why had I denied my fear of her? I should have simply said yes.

I rushed out of the room and sat down, my hands clammy. She slowly backed out, her silver-ringed fingers gripping the desk tightly. She moved a little further down the hall, ten feet or so behind me. Great, now I really wouldn't be able to focus. I would feel watched, hunted.

Mrs. Demmy came out, shook her gray-haired head at us, went back inside, and closed the door behind her.

Five minutes into the assignment, I hadn't completed anything. All I could think about was whether or not Samantha was watching me. Was she planning to kill me, or was she restarting her assignment to kill time? Was she going to try to give me the answers again? I didn't want them.

I nearly jumped out of my seat when something warm touched my back. I closed my eyes and inhaled. Silky black hair brushed against my cheek, and I realized that Samantha's large, soft breasts were pressing up against me. She leaned in closer, her minty breath against my ear, and slid the tip of her pencil down my arm, and onto number three of the assignment. Pins and needles descended into my groin area.

"You having trouble? This one's the hardest," she said.

"I..." was all I could say.

"Are you sure you aren't scared of me?" she asked.

Her voice was so soft, so seductive. I closed my eyes and thought I would faint. My cheeks burned and my palms moistened. I was speechless. Powerless. Vulnerable.

Instead of waiting for my response, she wrote a number and a name on the corner of my paper. A phone number. Her cell number? What was she doing? She could have taken a knife to my throat, and I wouldn't have cared right now. I was in heaven. I breathed in her perfume and closed my eyes.

"It's Friday; I'm having a party. Text me later and I'll tell you where to find me."

"Okay," was all I could say. My eyes glazed over.

She playfully squeezed my shoulders and walked away. I must have remained red in the face for nearly five minutes. All I wanted to do was jump into a swimming pool to cool off. I didn't get any of my work done. I simply stared at my paper.

"Well, I'm done," I heard her say behind me.

She stood up, pulled her desk back towards the classroom, and smiled at me one last time before disappearing. I slid my finger across her phone number and smiled to myself. I noticed that below her number, she had signed her name, "Sam." *Sam*, I thought dreamily.

Was this happening? Would I go to the party? Would I even have the guts to text her? There were so many thoughts flowing through my mind, I couldn't grasp any form of answer. We didn't speak again after I returned to the classroom. When the bell rang, I was scared to see her again in English, but at the same time, I couldn't wait.

I entered the classroom; however, she was nowhere to be seen. She had skipped, I assumed. Maybe she too was embarrassed by what had happened. Maybe it had been a dare? A dare to test my sexuality? Fury built up inside of me. I looked around, absolutely paranoid. Who else was in on this big joke? But there were no visible signs. Deep breaths. So maybe I was being paranoid.

I went home with a nasty feeling in my stomach, contemplating whether or not to text her. I lay on my bed, opening and closing my cell phone. I entered messages a few times but chickened out and closed my phone again. I conversed with myself, *Come on, Kaity, just text her. It's not a big deal. See what happens. If it's weird, you don't have to talk to her again. If you don't text her, you'll regret it for a long time, and you're always gonna wonder what could have happened.*

This was true. What was I supposed to do? Sit at home Friday night, wondering how Sam's party was going? It would be absolute torture. I opened my phone again and wrote,

"Hey, it's Kaitlyn. Still having a party?"

I entered her phone number and allowed my finger to hover over the send button for a few minutes, as I read, and reread the message to reassure my brain of its perfection. *Just send it!* And before I could think about it anymore, I quickly pressed down on "send." I wanted to cancel! What had I done? It was too late now.

Sam was going to receive my text, and I would have to go to the party. I felt queasy.

BEED-A-LEEP.

I quickly reopened the flap and read,

"Hey babe, of course. 117 Dolly Avenue, 8 p.m."

I sighed and held the phone over my heart. Yes!

Chapter 3

"Well, well, well," Sam said, opening the front door of her townhouse.

The neighborhood was a little rough, but the house itself looked quite nice. It had an old white-and-brown exterior, and a cute little pebble walkway leading to the front door. There was a small garden in front of the house; I could tell it hadn't been maintained. But that didn't matter. All I cared to look at was Sam. She was stunning as always, her style dark and her eyes s

"Hey," I mumbled, smiling up at her.

She took my jacket, hung it up, and led me into the kitchen, where the majority of her friends were hanging out. This was the strangest group of people I had ever seen. The ages must have varied from fifteen to fifty, and the styles found here were unique. Some men had long hair, while others had no hair. There were many piercings and tattoos all around.

"Here," Sam said, handing me a Budweiser.

"Oh, I... I don't drink," I said.

I sensed many eyes turn my way before a whole lot of laughter erupted around me.

"Guys, shut up!" Sam hissed at them.

She looked at me, much more warmly than she had anyone else in the room and asked, "You've never had a drink before?"

"N—No. Never, actually." I shrugged.

"It's not so bad. Here, try a sip. You'll make me happy," she said, smirking.

Make her happy? Great, now I had to try it. I couldn't say no. All I wanted was for Samantha Boward like me.

I grabbed the beer and tilted it slowly, sensing her intense eyes on me. When the bubbles reached my lips, I licked the droplets and pulled away. My face must have reflected my exact thoughts; Sam burst out laughing. I had never heard her laugh before. She had such a nice laugh.

"What?" I asked, grinning.

"You didn't like that so much, did you?"

I hated it. How did anyone drink beer? "It... it was okay," I lied.

"Kaity, no one likes beer their first time. You'll get used to it. The buzz is what counts anyway." She placed a hand on my shoulder.

Kaity? She called me Kaity, not Kaitlyn. I

loved it. I suddenly felt as though I'd known this girl for years.

"Okay," I said and took another sip.

"Good girl," she said.

I began to feel slightly light-headed halfway through my beer and realized that I enjoyed the sensation. I forcefully drank the rest of it, seeing as everyone else had downed their fifth beer.

Clush, I heard, and Sam had a fresh cold beer under my nose. I thanked her and grabbed it, but she didn't let go. She leaned in slowly, her cheek brushing against mine, and whispered in my ear, "At this rate, I might be able to take advantage of you by the end of the night."

I didn't know what to say. This was proof. She was a lesbian! What did that make me?

I laughed uncomfortably and drank some more, but she squeezed my arm and chuckled. "I'm teasing you, Kaity, relax. Stop being so tense."

All right, so maybe she wasn't a lesbian. She was teasing me, trying to help me discover myself, maybe. This was all so confusing. By my third beer, I was feeling pretty good. I made friends with a sixteen-year-old boy named Alex who was currently lining up coke on the living room table.

What a place, I thought, looking around.

Sam was chatting everyone up, *cheersing* anyone who held a beer bottle. I'd never felt this happy before. I felt so safe, so comfortable, as if nothing else in the world mattered but the present moment. It must have been the alcohol. I suddenly noticed Sam look my way. Her drunk, excited grin shortened into a more loving, compassionate smile. Was it real? I smiled back her way and shyly looked down at my beer.

Suddenly, explosive laughter caught my attention. I noticed a blond-haired man swing his arms around Sam, his large hands cupping her ass. I tensed. Was he going to hurt her? But I realized that it was she who was laughing. She aggressively pulled his hair and licked his throat, his chin, and his lips. The make-out session may have lasted a mere three seconds, but it felt like an eternity.

I became light-headed, nauseous, and shaky. This time it wasn't the alcohol. Jealousy? What the hell was this? She was allowed to kiss whoever she wanted. What did I care? But I couldn't control the rage. I stood up, put my beer down, and made my way to the foyer. As I slid on my jacket, Sam called my name. Ignoring it, I turned the door handle and pulled, but the door slammed shut before I had the time to fully open it.

Sam leaned against the door, staring at me.

"Where you going?"

"Home," I said.

"What the hell's wrong with you? We're having fun. Aren't you?" she asked. "Drink some more."

"I don't want to drink, Sam. I'm fine. Leave me alone." I tried to pull on the handle again, but her weight wouldn't allow it.

Her eyes narrowed into slits. "Are you jealous?"

I held back a scoff. "Jealous of what?"

My words were coming out with much more ease now. No more stuttering, no more blanking. The alcohol was improving my communication skills—or lack thereof, to be more accurate.

"Of Travis, the one I made out with," she said.

"Is he your boyfriend?" I asked.

I was coming across as the jealous girlfriend. What was I thinking? The words were spilling out, and my filter was no longer functioning.

"What does it matter? Are you my girlfriend?" she asked. I could sense that she too, was getting angry now.

I almost said, *It's kind of hard to date a straight girl*, but fortunately, I refrained from doing so. I would have regretted it in the morning. I opened my mouth, but closed it again and looked down at the floor. I didn't know what to say. I wanted to hug her, to hit her, and to cry, all at the same time. Was this the alcohol?

"I'm sorry," was all I could say.

She didn't respond. Instead, she walked away, freeing me from my captive state. I almost went back inside to talk to her some more, but I knew that it was pointless. So I zipped up my jacket and walked out in search of a taxi.

BEED-A-LEEP.

Adrenaline coursed through me. Sam. Please be Sam. But it was Matt: "What you doin?"

Great, I thought. But then I looked down at the time: 11:30 p.m. It was still early, considering it was Friday night. Did I want to go back home, drunk and alone? I needed to be surrounded by people, by noise, by anything. Instead of texting him back, I simply called.

"Hey, Matt."

"Heyyy! What're you doing? Come over. I'm having a party!" he shouted.

It was very difficult to hear him, what with the background music blasting and people shouting over one another. It was the perfect setting for my current condition. I knew where he lived, so I waved down a cab. I didn't want to spend the little bit of birthday savings I had, but

I didn't care at that moment.

"I'll be there soon, bye," I said and hung up.

When I arrived at his house, it was precisely what I had expected, and more. Everyone was drunk, the music was blaring, and there were shot glasses all over the place. Where his parents were, I don't quite remember. I'm not even sure that he mentioned it. And I didn't care. I enjoyed myself, met new people, and, well, got smashed for the first time in my life.

*   *   *

I woke up, unfortunately. My head throbbed and my stomach felt as though it had shrunk down three sizes. My entire back was painfully stiff, and my legs ached. What the hell had I done? I retraced my steps:

Sam's party, the fight, leaving.

Arrival at Matt's party.

Beer.

Shots.

Conversations I couldn't remember.

Crying on someone's shoulder.

A taxi ride.

… This morning.

Wow. What a nasty feeling. What if I'd done something terrible? Had I kissed anyone? Had I had sex with Matt? No, I couldn't have. No drug in the world would have ever led to that. I was panicking. I was so ashamed, so fearful, so guilty of the unknown.

BEED-A-LEEP.

Oh, just what I needed right now. I moaned as I reached over to grab my phone, cotton-mouthed and dizzy. Text from Matt:

"Thx for comin last nite, had lots of fun. U need to drink more often, haha!"

What the hell was that supposed to mean? Oh no, I had done something, hadn't I? Just as I closed my phone, a message flashed on the front screen. "Three missed calls." One was from Matt, but the other two were from Sam later that night. She had tried calling after I left! It was a good sign, I thought.

My Saturday afternoon consisted mainly of curing my hangover, explaining to my parents that I had tried alcohol for the first time (there was no hiding it), and contemplating whether or not to text Sam or to return her phone call. I felt better by supper time, which sucked seeing as my parents would be ready to interrogate me.

We all sat around the dinner table, more silent than usual, and the questioning began. I answered as best as I could, defending myself with the use of the "I'm a teenager; it's normal to experiment" line. But the subject changed rather abruptly when my mother smiled and sat up straight.

"Kaity, I have good news," she said.

I gawked around and caught my sister

smiling at me. What was this all about? Before my mother could explain herself, Amy jumped in, "Andrew's cousin, Gabriel, is moving to Loshano next week. He's gorgeous, and I want you to meet him."

"You're setting me up?" I asked.

"Yeah! I'm telling you, I think you two will hit it off," Amy said.

Her excitement was real, as was my mother's. I inhaled deeply and stared at my plate. I didn't want to be set up. I wanted Sam. I wanted the feeling of Sam's warm, naked body against mine; her soft lips against my neck; her delicate hands on my stomach. I was finally beginning to admit the truth to myself.

"Kaity?" my mother asked, confused by my reaction—or lack of reaction, I should say.

I looked up at her, at my father, and then at Amy. Why were they trying so desperately? Why did it matter to them whether or not I had a boyfriend? I didn't want to deliberately hurt any one of them, but their attempts to make me *normal* in their eyes were a rejection of my true self. I was the victim here. Without giving it a second thought, I pulled my chair back, rested my utensils against the plate, and stood up. My mother looked up at me with worried eyes, but I didn't allow emotion to get in the way.

"Look, I appreciate what you guys are doing. But I think you all know the truth, and you're all in denial." And with that, I walked away. I couldn't believe I'd said it.

"Sweetheart!" my mother called out, and I looked back.

She was smiling. Was she accepting that I didn't like boys?

"What are you talking about?" she asked, eyebrows furrowed.

I sighed. Was she truly confused or was she ignorantly refusing to believe?

"Seriously?" I asked.

She didn't answer but simply waited. My dad stared at his plate, disgusted by what I had just said. He didn't bother to deny it—he knew. Amy's eyes shot back and forth between my mother and me.

I knew I would have to be blunt to break through her barrier of denial. So I said it. "Mom, I'm gay. I'm a lesbian. Okay? Just accept it. I don't want to date Gabriel or any other male on this planet." And with that, I left.

I heard my mother sob as I walked up to my room. What had I done? I suddenly realized that voicing my sexuality had removed a great weight from my shoulders. How had I not seen it? How had I honestly believed I was straight? All of these years? Denial was a powerful defense mechanism, I realized.

But in that very moment, as I thought about Sam, there was no doubt in my mind that I,

Kaitlyn Noles, was attracted to women. I wasn't afraid to admit it anymore. I was so tired of hiding from everyone—of finding excuses as to why I had never had sex with a boy, why I'd always get nervous around girls, and why I would always catch myself staring down the shirts of my waitresses or admiring their curves from behind as they walked away. Gay, gay, gay, gay, gay!

When the rush finally faded, I was alone—alone in my room with my lonesome thoughts. What now? My family hated me. My mother was disgusted, and my father was ashamed. And Amy, well, she was the straightest, most homophobic woman I knew! I was screwed.

Ignoring the fight I had had with Sam the night before, I opened my phone and prepared a text: "I told my parents I'm gay. They hate me now."

Should I send it to Sam, I wondered? Maybe she would help me. I needed someone right now. Whether or not she was also gay didn't matter. She accepted it, and that was all that mattered. I hit send. The five-minute wait felt like an hour. But, the sound I was waiting for echoed by my side.

BEED-A-LEEP.

Her reply read: "Come over, bring extra clothes."

I couldn't believe it. She was going to help

me. She must have forgotten about last night. I jumped out of bed and stuffed a bunch of clothes, my makeup, and a toothbrush into my backpack. This was it. I was running away. An eighteen-year-old runaway—a little late, I thought, smiling to myself.

I didn't bother climbing out of a window. Instead, I walked downstairs, head held high, and walked right out through the front door. They wouldn't try to stop me, I knew. They wanted me out. I hopped on a city bus and eventually found my way to 117 Dolly Avenue.

"Hey," Sam said, beer bottle in hand as she opened the front door. It was six-thirty p.m. and she was still wearing pajamas.

I walked in, smiling pathetically. I felt so defeated, standing there with a bag of clothes.

"Grab a beer in the fridge; you'll feel better," she said.

I did exactly that—and, well, I did feel much better.

"So, you're a lesbian," she said, smirking.

I shrugged and looked away.

"Kaity, stop it," she said much more sternly than I'd ever heard her speak to me before.

"Stop what?" I said. I was nervous again.

"Stop acting like you've committed a crime. You're a lesbo, so what? We're in the twenty-first century. Everyone's coming out." She laughed.

What a relief. I sipped my beer, smiled at her shyly, and nodded.

"Come here," she said.

I widened my eyes. Come here? Where? We were seated on a three-seat sofa, one cushion apart. How much closer did she want me?

"Come beside me, see what it feels like."

"What? No," I said and laughed uncomfortably. "That's retarded."

She stretched her body across the sofa and extended an inviting arm. I wanted nothing more than to lie down beside her, against her, but I couldn't move.

"I'm not being sexual; I'm being a friend. Come lie with me, you'll like it, I promise," she said.

I awkwardly crawled over to her side and lay rigidly beside her, trying to keep at least an inch of distance between us. But she wrapped her arm around my neck and pulled me in closer, forcing my cheek to rest against her breast.

"Stop it," she said.

"Stop what?" I laughed.

"Stop pushing me away. Relax. It's not every day that a babe like me will ask you to do something like this." She burst out laughing.

I chuckled.

"Yeah, I guess you're right," I said.

I took a deep breath and closed my eyes. My

arms were stiff by my side. This would have looked extremely graceless to anyone observing. I finally began to relax a little, and I hesitantly slid my arm across her stomach. I flinched when she grabbed that arm and forced it tight around her waist, but I didn't move from my new position. Instead, I enjoyed the warmth of her body against mine and the soft pillow of flesh against my face.

"Are you comfortable?" she asked.

"Yeah," I breathed.

"Good."

We both fell asleep that way, beer bottles in hand.

Chapter 4

"Wake up, you lovebirds!"

I jolted upright and backed away from Sam as if I had been caught doing something wrong. She slowly sat up and shoved me to the other side of the couch jokingly.

"Get the hell off of me, you rapist! You criminal!" she shouted, then jumped on top of me and began smothering me with sofa cushions.

I laughed and fought back, enjoying every second of my playful beating. I realized that the boy—or man—was still staring at us, smiling.

"Sam, are you done?" he asked.

She jumped off me, reached for her pack of cigarettes on the table, and said, "Yeah, I'm done. What do you want, Travis?"

Travis! Her boyfriend! I suddenly wanted to punch him. He had that same shaggy blond hair as I remembered, and a very rugged style. He was thin, but tall and handsome. This was the guy she had made out with. I hadn't noticed I was glaring at him until Sam turned around, smiled at me, and said, "Kaity, relax. This is my roommate, he's not my boyfriend."

I tried to act innocent—careless. I shrugged and raised my eyebrows.

"Wouldn't matter if he was," I said.

"Yeah, yeah, shut up." She lit her smoke and took a sip of beer.

"I'm going downtown right now. What do you want me to get you?" Travis asked.

"Um," Sam said and looked back at me. "Get me two two-fours, same stuff; Kaity's having a rough day." She reached for her wallet and handed Travis eighty dollars.

He shoved the money in his back pocket and left the room.

"You fine with beer?" she asked.

"Um, yeah, I don't really care," I said.

"Well, drink up," she said, *cheersed* me, and chugged the remainder of her Bud.

I forced the rest of mine down and placed the empty on the table.

"Shit!" Sam suddenly said. "Travis, wait up!"

She rushed out the front door, but was back within ten seconds.

"What was that?" I asked.

"Ever tried lime-flavored beer?" she asked.

"No," I said. Lime-flavored? That sounded

odd.

"You'll like it better. Travis is going to pick some up for you," she said.

"Oh, you didn't have to..." I said.

"Shush... here." She handed me another full beer.

I smirked. "Thanks."

We sat in silence for a while, sipping here and there. I zoned out, reminding myself of how great it felt to lie beside her, and whether or not she would ever let me do that again.

"Kaity?" she asked.

I looked at her. Her expression was suddenly serious—unreadable. I swallowed but didn't speak.

"Do you want to kiss me?" she asked.

My face, neck, and chest lit up a tomato red. I couldn't believe she had asked me that.

"What? Why? Why would you ask me that?" I stuttered.

"Well, do you?" she asked.

How could she be so direct? Had she no shame? No filter? Was she still teasing me? What the hell was she doing?

"Yes or no, Kaity," she said, glaring at me now.

I burst into uncomfortable laughter and shrugged.

"Am I making you uncomfortable?" she asked, tilting her head.

"Yeah, I mean, a bit," I said.

I couldn't look at her. My face was on fire. I hoped that the lighting in this room wasn't bright enough for her to notice.

"Stop it," she said.

I smiled. "Stop what?" I asked, raising my eyes to meet hers.

She reached an open hand out and stared at me until I finally grabbed it. She pulled me in one cushion closer, right beside her. I didn't realize how heavily I was breathing until she pointed it out.

"Why are you so nervous around me?" she asked.

"I... I don't know," I said.

I honestly didn't know where these nerves were coming from. Our hands were still locked together, and our thighs were touching. I flinched back when she pressed an open palm against my chest.

"Wow, will you relax? I'm not gonna hurt you."

So I sat still, holding her hand, and feeling slightly light-headed. Maybe it was the beer; maybe it was the butterflies—I was unable to differentiate the two.

"Holy shit. I really do make you uncomfortable," she said. "Your heart's racing like crazy."

"No," I said.

"No? You're perfectly comfortable with me right now?" She stared at me, but I looked down through the neck of my beer bottle.

"Stop it," she said.

I laughed and rolled my eyes.

"Stop what?" I asked stupidly.

I hadn't had the time to do or say anything else. Her face approached me and I felt her soft, pink lips press up against mine. My eyes involuntarily closed and my entire body tingled. I was anything but tense.

I suddenly felt as though I would collapse and splash like Jello on her carpet floor. Our lips didn't separate for a few seconds, and every one of those seconds was perfect. She slowly pulled away and observed me for a moment. My dreamy eyes and half-open mouth must have shown her how much I truly enjoyed it; she suddenly grinned and started singing, "You kissed a girl, and you liked it."

I laughed and leaned my head against her shoulder. "Yeah, I did."

"It's okay." She raised my chin with the tips of her fingers. "There's nothing wrong with that."

I smiled, but not for long. There was something I had wanted to ask her for a very long time, and I needed an answer.

"Sam?" I asked.

"Yeah, babe?" she said, teasingly.

"Are you gay? I mean, are you messing with me, or?"

"What does it matter to you?" she asked.

"I don't know; it just does." I didn't know how to express myself.

"Do you want me to be gay?" she asked.

"Stop it," I was the one to say this time.

"Stop what?" She stuck her tongue out at me.

"Well, you made out with..." I said.

"Kaity, making out with a boy when I'm drunk doesn't mean I like him. He's my roommate. We're friends. I do stupid shit all the time."

"Which kiss was better?" I asked.

"I think we both know the answer to that," she said

She leaned in and kissed me again. This was heaven. I hoped to stay here with her forever. I wanted to forget school, to forget my family, to forget everything and everyone but Sam.

"Come here," she said, lying down again.

I didn't hesitate this time. I crawled into her arms and huddled close—I was the little spoon. She reached over me and grabbed the TV's remote control. Together, we watched different shows and movies for hours, until nightfall came. I had never done that before. I had never had the patience to sit through one movie, let alone hours of TV. But it wasn't the

TV that I cared for. I enjoyed her warmth against my back and the heartbeat from her chest.

"Hey, Sam. Who's your friend?" I heard someone ask from a distance.

I didn't realize that I had fallen asleep. I kept my eyes closed and listened.

"Is she sleeping?" Sam whispered from behind me.

The other person, a female, didn't respond. She must have nodded.

"A friend from school," Sam said.

A friend? Just a friend? But what was I expecting? I wasn't her girlfriend. She was, after all, just a friend. I was being sensitive. I didn't move.

"She's cute. You like her?" her friend whispered.

This was it! I was *asleep*, therefore, Sam had no reason to lie.

"Fuck off," Sam laughed.

What did that mean? Was I supposed to feel like a joke? Because I did. Was her friend teasing her, knowing that Sam wasn't gay? Or, maybe Sam was gay, and she didn't want to admit to liking me. I hoped that the latter was the reason for her defensive response. I hoped so much.

"You got my cut?" Sam asked.

"Yeah, four hundred. I'll leave it on your

dresser."

"Thanks, Mel," Sam said.

"No problem."

And silence returned. Sam tightened her arm around my waist, her breasts pressing up against my back. She liked me; she had to! A burst of emotions rushed through me, and I wanted to smile, but didn't want to give away my *fake-sleeping* ruse. I danced inside, only inside, but all thought ceased when Sam's lips tickled my ear.

"You are kind of cute, you sneaky little shit," she whispered.

Crap. Did she know I was awake? No, she was testing me. I didn't move.

"I know you're awake," she said, trying not to laugh.

Don't give in! Don't give in! I thought loudly.

"All right, you want to play?" she asked.

She slid her hand down my side and over my thigh and slowly made her way down to my pelvic area. I felt her fingers crawl underneath the elastic of my pants and a sudden tingling of warmth shot to my groin. I burst into excited laughter, grabbed her wrist, and swung around to face her.

"Okay, you win!" I shouted.

"I always win," she said.

She pulled her wrist free and began pinching any part of me that she could grab. It was unbearable, but her laughter was contagious. I tried to fight back, but instead, pulled backward and fell off of the couch right onto my back. A loud *thump* echoed throughout the living room, and my breath was forced out of my lungs. Her head popped out into the open and she looked down at me, her long, silky straight hair tickling the tip of my nose.

"You okay?" she snorted.

"I'm good," I said, looking up at her.

"Get back up here; I'll be nice," she said.

I climbed back up onto the couch and sat at the other end, my feet against her thighs for my own safety.

"How'd you know I wasn't sleeping?" I asked.

"I know things," she said, a sly smile forming at the corner of her lips.

"Come on, tell me."

She threw her head back and laughed. The answer was obvious, I assumed.

"Kaity, your heart was racing like crazy when Mel walked in. What were you expecting to hear?" she asked.

"I don't know," I said, shrugging.

"Liar."

"I'm not sure!" I said. She was making me nervous again. She had this way of prying, of picking at me until I surrendered.

"Do you think I like you?" she asked, no hint

of humor in the tone of her voice.

Shit. This was it—the big trap. I was about to receive the "we're just friends, I hope you know that" speech. I didn't want to hear it. I wouldn't fall victim to that embarrassment.

"No, of course not," I said, shaking my head.

Her eyes remained fixed on me a little longer than I had hoped. I looked away. She stood up and made her way to the kitchen, grabbed a phone, and looked back at me.

"I'm ordering pizza. What do you want?" she asked.

She was torturing me! Why these mind games? She was so straightforward about anything... and everything, but when it came down to actual emotion, she'd walk away or change the subject. Gah!

"Doesn't matter," I said, honestly.

"No, pick something," she said.

"Um, pepperoni is fine," I said.

But this decision had somehow upset her. She bowed her head forward quietly, squeezed the bridge of her nose, and sniffled softly. Her lip quivered.

"Sam?" I asked.

She shook her lowered head and sobbed, now covering her entire face with her hands and phone.

"Sam, what did I say? What's wrong?"

"How could you eat a living creature?" she

asked. "I know they're not humans, but they have feelings too. I thought you were more sensitive than that, Kaity," she said and exhaled a loud, quivering breath.

I didn't hesitate. I rushed forward to her and placed my hand on her shoulder, but she pulled away. I felt like such an asshole.

"Sam, I didn't know you were a vegetarian. I'm sorry. I'm really sorry. Order a vegetarian pizza. I like that too."

"What? So now you think that an apology will fix all of the animal flesh you've ever eaten? It doesn't work that way, Kaity," she said.

Wow, this girl was passionate, not to mention emotional. I hated to be the reason for her anger. All I wanted to do was fix what I'd done, but I didn't know what to say. I felt my face go red yet again, and I awkwardly rubbed her shoulder.

"I'm really sorry; I am," was all I could manage.

"Just fucking with you," Sam said, suddenly jolting upright and grinning at me. "Pepperoni's my favorite. You should have seen your face." She burst out laughing.

Although slightly irritated by the fact that I had fallen victim to one of her games, I couldn't help but smile. She knew how to have fun.

"You're psychotic," I said, shaking my head.

She laughed again, directly in my face this

time, and dialed a number on her phone.

"Watch this," she said. She was so exciting—so daring.

"Hello?" she said in a very nasally kind of voice. "Yesss... I have a bad hip, so I thought I vould call first to see if you have vat I'm looking forrr."

I threw my hands over my mouth to keep quiet. Her voice was priceless. She laughed away from the phone then returned and forced herself to regain composure.

"Yes... I'm looking for a vibranimanator. I heard you're the only shop in Loshano who carries dat."

Again, she pulled away, her eyes closed tightly and her face reddening.

"Pizza? No, I've tried with da pizza before, it burnt more dan anything. No! No pizza! What kind of a sex shop is this? Gad, you are so stoopid!" and she hung up.

She was fascinating. I watched as she cramped over and laughed and laughed and laughed.

"Did you...?" she tried. "Did you like that?" she finally managed to ask me.

I couldn't respond. It had been extremely funny, but I had much more enjoyed watching her have so much fun. Although completely out of my nature, I grabbed her face and kissed her hard.

Chapter 5

"What was that for?" she asked.

The laughter had ceased, and she looked at me as if I'd lost my way in the West Edmonton Mall.

"I'm not sure. An urge, I'm sorry. I won't do it again," I said.

She lowered her eyebrows and gawked at me.

"Why are you sorry? You can do that anytime you want," she said, before dialing another number and turning away.

She ordered pepperoni pizza before grabbing another round of beers out of the fridge. Anytime I wanted? She hadn't joked this time. We returned to the sofa and sat down.

As she surfed the channels, she stared intently at the TV and said, "I think you like me."

"What? Why do you say that?" I asked.

"Why don't you just admit it?" She turned towards me.

"Why don't you?" I asked.

She hadn't much liked that comment, because she rolled her eyes and proceeded to scan the TV channels. My heart raced and I swallowed the thick lump in my throat. Why couldn't I admit it? I did like her. I did. But it was all so much at once. I'd only just come out to my parents that day, and now, what? Was I supposed to understand everything about lesbianism? I needed help with this. I was so lost.

"I'm not used to this. I'm sorry," I said.

I stared at the carpet shamefully, embarrassed by my feelings for her. She tossed the remote aside and sat upright, legs crossed. She reached out her hand, and I didn't hesitate to grab it.

"You like me; say it," she said. "You'll feel better."

I didn't understand why she wanted me to say it first. What if I agreed to it, only to be rejected? Only to be crushed for the first time? She must have sensed my fear; she squeezed my hand and looked at me with sympathy.

"I'm not going to shoot you down," she said.

Well then, what was the big deal? This would all have been so much easier had she admitted to liking me first. But I realized that

Samantha Boward wasn't the type to follow. She was a leader; a dominant. And someone like her didn't take rejection lightly. This was her way of protecting herself. So, I submitted to her.

"I like you," I finally said, "a lot."

I hadn't noticed that my hands were shaking until she cupped them with both of hers. "Relax. Calm down, babe."

I simply nodded, awaiting my rejection. Take it like a man, I thought humorously, taking a deep breath.

"Come on, are you that naive?" she asked. This caught my attention. What was that supposed to mean?

"I think it's pretty obvious that I like you too, Kaity," she said.

And there it was—absolute freedom. The weight had been lifted! I exhaled loudly and leaned in for a hug. The moment was so liberating. It was ecstasy. We didn't speak afterward. We simply held onto each other until eventually, the doorbell rang.

"Must be the pizza guy," she said and rushed to the front door.

The delicious smell of melted cheese and pepperoni slices filled the house, and we huddled over the open box, savoring every bite. Halfway through our meal, Travis came back home.

"Here ya go, girls," he said, placing two twenty-fours of Budweiser by the sofa, along with a small six-pack of Bud Light Lime.

Sam pulled out a lime beer, cracked it open with her hands, and offered it to me. She watched as I slowly sipped and smiled with anticipation.

"Well?" she asked.

Wow. That was delicious. This was so much better than regular beer.

"That's amazing," I blurted out.

She laughed at what I assumed were my facial expressions, and I drank some more. I definitely felt a buzz, and I loved it. Why had I waited so long to begin drinking?

We finished our pizza and Sam leaned back against the sofa's armrest.

"Let's play a drinking game," she said.

A drinking game? I would need coaching.

"How do we play?" I asked.

"Simple. Deck of cards: one through six is the number of chugs the other person has to take. Anything above six results in a truth question," she said.

"Um. I don't get it."

"Look." She grabbed a deck of cards from the table (apparently they enjoyed playing cards often) and shuffled it quickly. She placed the pile facedown on the floor and turned over the first card. A nine of spades.

"So, seeing as the number is higher than six, I get to ask you any question I want. If you don't want to answer it, you have to chug your entire beer."

"What? That's insane," I said.

"Well then, be sure to answer," she said and flipped another card. Three of diamonds. "Now, because this card is below six, you have to take three shots, well, gulps, of your beer. Had it been a four, you'd have taken four shots. No pussy sips either. It has to be a mouthful."

"Oh okay. I get it. That sounds like fun. What about six? Is that a question, or..."

"Six shots."

"Gotcha," I said.

"Let us begin. You can start," she said, rubbing her palms together.

I flipped: seven of hearts.

"So, I ask you something?" I asked.

"Yup."

"Like what?"

This was a little harder than I had expected. I wasn't very skilled at coming up with ideas on the spot.

"Anything. Favorite this, favorite that. Past experiences. Future hopes. Whatever," she said.

I pondered for a bit, chewing on my fingernail. And then something came up.

"Where do you work?"

"I don't," she said, smiling.

"Well, then how do you?" I said.

"Ah, ah, ah. One question per turn, cheater."

I rolled my eyes and smiled.

"Go," I said.

She flipped: two of spades.

"Drink up," she said, and I did.

The game went on for a few hours, and by the end of it, I was slurring and my vision had doubled. But, we had learned many facts about each other. What I remembered as most important in my book of facts about Samantha Boward, was this:

She was completely gay.

She didn't want to discuss her parents.

She didn't want to discuss her living situation.

She wasn't a virgin.

She didn't want to discuss how she made money.

And what she knew about me, was this:

I was completely gay.

I lived with both of my parents and my sister.

I wanted to become a Science teacher.

I was a virgin.

I had no job and barely any money.

The fact that she hadn't wanted to discuss anything of importance led me to believe that there was something to hide. I didn't want to pry, because I didn't want her to dislike me or feel any form of anger towards me.

She tossed the cards aside and yawned, grabbed my hand, and stood up.

"Come here," she said, leading me out of the living room.

I stumbled a few times, laughed it off, and looked ahead. This was fantastic. I loved being drunk. I felt so powerful—so unstoppable. Anything and everything I did or said would be accepted, because it just had to be.

Before I knew it, we were lying in her bed, side by side. Moonlight illuminated her face through the blinds, and I could tell she was smiling, but not as I had ever seen her do before. Her eyes scanned my body and returned to my face.

"What?" I asked.

No response.

"Sam?"

Her soft fingers wrapped around my wrist, and my hand was pulled towards her stomach, underneath her shirt, and up towards her bra cup. What was she doing? Don't get me wrong, I was enjoying this, but I had never touched another woman before.

"It's okay," she whispered.

I had wanted to pull away, but my lack of inhibition let me continue. I rubbed my thumb gently underneath the cup of her bra, feeling the soft flesh of her breast.

"You can take it off," she said, "and do whatever you want with me."

And although I did not have sex with Samantha Boward that night, I spent what felt like hours touching every inch of her body—gliding my fingers against her soft delicate flesh; along the ridges of her hip bones; around the goose-bumped curves of her waist; and atop the smooth, shaven skin of her legs.

Chapter 6

Morning arrived rather unforgivingly. I sat upright in Sam's bed and rubbed my crusted eyes. Where was I? When had I fallen asleep? I looked around and noticed the digital clock at the corner of her bedside table: 3:34 p.m. What? How the hell had I managed to sleep so late? I had never slept in this late. Ten a.m., to me, was sleeping in.

I threw my legs over the edge of the bed as if in a hurry to attend to something of importance. What was I rushing to? I wasn't certain at the moment. But, then it hit me. I ran to find the bathroom and dropped my head into the toilet bowl. Fluid came pouring right out of me—that's right, fluid. Acid. There was no food; I simply gagged and gagged and gagged, hoping that I would soon die.

"You all right, kid?" I heard Sam ask.

I looked up and wiped the acidic drool from

my lips. Sam. I suddenly felt comforted. I tried to smile, but I must have grimaced because she laughed and handed me a glass of water.

"Here, you'll need that. Let me get you a beer, too. It'll help."

And I threw up again. A beer. That was the last thing I wanted right now. This girl was insane. I closed my eyes and rested my head along the edge of the toilet bowl. Calmness. Peace. Sleep.

"Hey, wake up."

My eyes lazily opened again.

"Here, drink up. Seriously, trust me," Sam said.

I moaned and turned my head away. I didn't want beer! I wanted a cure.

"Kaity, stop it," she said.

I tried to reply, but instead coughed up some more acid and growled. She laughed at me, a subtle tone of sympathy in her voice, and rubbed my arm.

"You have to trust me. If it doesn't work, I'll let you rape me."

At this, I released a weak laugh. I looked up at her from the toilet bowl—pathetically I'm sure, forced a smile, and said, "Well that's dumb. It's a win-win."

"She still has a sense of humor!" Sam said and handed me the beer.

To be honest, it took a few attempts to keep

the liquid down. After a few more toilet bowl visits, I finally managed to drink half of it. Was I cured? No. But the dizziness faded and my insides calmed themselves.

"Keep going. There's more where that came from," she said.

She was right. By the end of my beer, I felt much better. Who in their right mind had discovered this hangover trick? *Oh, I feel so terrible, so sick—therefore, I must have another drink!* It didn't make any sense to me whatsoever, but hey, it worked.

"You want to order some nachos?" she asked, grinning at me.

At this point, my hunger had returned, and I was ready to give the day another shot. I stared at her for a moment, noting the excitement in her eyes, and tilted my head.

"Is that all you do?" I asked.

"What do you mean?" she asked.

"Order takeout? Don't you cook?" I asked.

She laughed at me as if I were five years old. "Silly, I can't cook. Besides, takeout is so good."

True enough, I thought.

"Today's Sunday, so, I think Sir Larry's is open for delivery," she mumbled to herself.

Sunday? Shit! I had school the next day. I couldn't spend another day drinking, eating takeout, and watching TV with Sam.

"I have to go home," I blurted, rising onto

my unsteady legs.

"Whoa. Hold on Kaity." She grabbed my arm and forced me back down. "What's the hurry?"

"I have school tomorrow. My parents. I haven't even talked to them. They don't know where I am. They could call the police. I can't skip school. They'll call my house. I... I... I'm already in so much shit."

"Kaity, shut up," she said.

I realized that I had been ranting. I had fallen into panic mode. But it was all true. I couldn't *not* go to school. And I had to let my parents know where I was. For all they knew, I had been kidnapped and tortured. Loshano was a decent-sized city—anything could happen.

"School," I said.

"Fuck school. You can take a day off. Stay with me. We'll go together on Tuesday. And you're eighteen, I don't think your parents need to know where you are every damned minute," she said.

One day missed couldn't be so bad, could it? I observed her suggestive eyes and stared at my empty beer bottle. What the hell. I had never skipped before. One day of being badass would do me some good. Before I could respond verbally, she squeezed my hand and said, "That a girl!"

But I still had a problem—my parents. Were they even worried? Did they even want me to return home? There was only one way to find out. I asked Sam to go find me my cell phone, and she was back within minutes, cell phone in one hand, and another beer in the other. I laughed and grabbed them both. Eleven missed calls from home. I had set myself up for a speech. Fortunately, I didn't have voice mail, so there would be no time wasted going through nasty messages.

"Promise me you won't say a word," I said, pointing a stiff finger at Sam.

"Why would I?" she asked.

"I'm putting it on speakerphone so you can hear my mom," I said.

"Yes!" she said, clapping her hands. "Not a word. Go on. Call her!"

I dialed, hit speaker, and placed the phone at the edge of my feet.

"Hello?" Amy answered.

"Hey, Amy, is Mom home?"

"Kaity?" Amy asked.

"Yeah, can I talk to Mom, please?"

No response.

"Hello?" my mom came on.

"Hey, Mom. Sorry I missed your calls. I left my phone at a friend's place."

"Oh, sweetheart..." I could tell she was choking up.

"So, how are you?" I asked.

There would be no time for chitchat. She

would jump right to it. I knew her.

"Kaity, listen. Your dad and I have been talking. We want you back here, but we've set some ground rules."

"Ground rules?" I asked. I looked up at Sam, whose expression resembled mine.

"You can't bring any girls here, and we'd like for you to attend weekly meetings at the community church. They can help you. We can change this... this..."

"Mom!"

"Oh, Kaity. You know God can save you. Have faith in him, please."

"Mom!"

"Kaity..."

"No! It doesn't work like that! There's nothing wrong with me! If there is a God, he made me this way, so stop trying to change it!" I snapped. I wanted to smash my phone into a million pieces. How could she be so ignorant? How could my entire family be so stupid? "Listen, I'm not coming home. If you guys can't accept that I'm not diseased, that this isn't a sin, then I want nothing to do with you."

"Kaity, please!"

"No! I love you guys, but I can't stand you right now. Bye." I hung up.

I hadn't had the time to look up at Sam, because she wrapped her arms around my neck and pulled me in close. I realized that my hands were shaking uncontrollably, and I was crying into the crease of her neck.

"It's okay, babe," she whispered. "I'm so sorry."

My crying amounted to shameless bawling. I tried to catch my breath, but it seemed impossible. She held me tighter. I grabbed handfuls of her T-shirt and squeezed her in closer. I had no one. No one but Sam. My own family thought me ill. Where would I go now? Who would take care of me? I was homeless. Why had I come out? I should have kept my big mouth shut. I suddenly felt a wave of anger towards Sam. This was her fault. It was her fault I'd begun to question my sexuality. My tight hold suddenly grew into aggressive pushing and shoving, but she locked my wrists together.

"Stop it!" she yelled, and she meant it. I had never heard her get angry, and it weakened me instantly.

"Don't be mad at me! I didn't force you to be a lesbian. I didn't force you to tell your parents. I'm here to help you, Kaity. I'm not trying to bring you down. So just stop it!"

Her black-outlined eyes were so menacing, so dominant.

She knew exactly what I was thinking, and that frightened me. She seemed to know everything. And she was right. Had she not been the one to slap reality into me, to bring forth the truth, it would have been someone else, or eventually, myself. But it was so much easier to blame someone else for what I felt was an injustice.

"I know it isn't easy, but we'll get through it, okay?" she reassured me.

"Sam, I barely even know you," I cried.

"Who cares?" she said. She grabbed my chin and forced my wet eyes to look up at her. "I like you, so I'll help you. And I don't like many people," she added jokingly.

At this, I smiled and nodded.

"Now drink up," she said. "We have a lot to forget."

I crawled my way up and followed her into the living room, from where we ordered Sir Larry's cheese nachos for breakfast. As nasty as that sounds, it was the most incredible breakfast I'd ever had. I was starving by the time it arrived, and a new buzz had begun to take over my body. I didn't give a shit about anything. I would enjoy my Sunday spent with Sam, and not worry about school; not worry about my family; and most of all, not give a damn about tomorrow.

By eight o'clock, we had finished twelve beers together, and we were both having a blast. Everything was funny. We watched Ellen DeGeneres on TV and danced with her, then cried together when she helped a single mother out of debt.

"Someday, I'm going to help people the way she does," Sam said.

And I believed her. I, too, had dreamed of being that famous someday, of having the financial ability to help those in need. I sipped some more beer and picked at the dried-up nachos on the living room table.

"You hungry again?" she asked.

"I'm not sure," I said and laughed.

So this time, we ordered cheese sticks and jalapeño poppers. Where she received the money to eat this much takeout was beyond me. I had promised myself not to bring it up again, but when Travis walked in and handed her a six hundred-dollar stack of twenty-dollar bills, I broke my promise.

"Why don't you tell me what you do? It isn't going to change the way I feel about you," I said. I was already beginning to slur, but I meant every word of what I was saying.

"Yeah, it will," she said.

She looked ashamed—afraid of what the truth might cause. I didn't care what she was or what she did (well, to an extent). I liked her, and that was all that mattered. Wasn't it?

"You aren't a prostitute, are you?" I asked, now slightly worried by her silence. I couldn't stand the thought of her being sexual with anyone else. Even the thought of her lying naked next to a stranger or undressing for someone caused my stomach to churn.

"Shut the fuck up," she said and shoved me jokingly.

"Phew," I said. "Well, if that isn't what you do, then whatever it is really doesn't matter."

For once, I was the one staring at her, apparently causing a certain level of discomfort. She opened her mouth, but then looked away.

"Come on, Sam, please."

"I don't do anything," she said.

"That doesn't make any sense. If you don't do..." I started.

"I honestly don't do anything. I get a cut of what Travis and Mel make because I give them a place to stash their drugs," she said, still shamefully staring at the ground.

I stared, processing what she had said. Was she telling the truth? Was she expecting me to feel repulsed? Was I supposed to be upset with her? In all honesty, I didn't care. If anything, it was easy money and I was jealous.

"That's it?" I asked. She finally glanced up at me.

"What do you mean, 'That's it'?" she asked.

"It doesn't sound like a big deal. You're not doing anything illegal, right? I mean, they're the ones selling."

She chortled and said, "Please, Kaity, spare

me. What I'm doing is extremely illegal."

Well, this was news to me. I wasn't very educated in the field of drugs. I looked down. I didn't know what to say. I didn't so much care that she was committing a crime, what bothered me was the thought of her getting punished for it. I didn't want her to end up in prison.

"Are you going to get caught?" I asked.

"Doubt it," she said and knocked on wood.

Lost for words, I simply leaned in and kissed her cheek.

"I still like you," I said, "a lot."

She looked at me, an alien shyness in her eyes, and smirked.

"Thanks," she said.

I excitedly jumped on top of her and pinned her down, which of course, evolved into a much more aggressive play fight. By the time the cheese sticks and poppers arrived, we were drunk again. So the food tasted that much better.

As I hung melted cheese over my tongue, I noticed that Sam wasn't eating, but instead, picking at her food.

"What's wrong?" I asked.

"I know we haven't known each other long at all, but you have nowhere to go. I'm not a U-Haul lesbian," she said and laughed, "but you could stay here until you figure everything out."

"A U-Haul lesbian?" I asked.

She chuckled cutely and swallowed a whole cheese stick.

"You gonna stay or not?"

Chapter 7

When I woke up dizzy the next morning, I hadn't the slightest idea whether staying with Samantha Boward was the right thing to do. Truthfully, the idea of moving in with her went against all that I had ever been taught about relationships:

Moving in with a friend usually led to disaster.

Moving in with a fresh crush was bound to cause a split.

Jumping in without first looking usually led to a cracked skull.

But, I had no other choice. Besides, I wouldn't stay for long, I assured myself. I would only stay until things fell into place for me.

"You can have that dresser. We'll go buy you some new clothes," she said, pointing to the corner of her room.

It was a tiny, auburn-colored thing with two

drawers and enough space on it to place an alarm clock.

"Sam, you don't have to," I said.

"Shush."

"At least let me get a job and help pay rent," I offered. And I'd meant it—I would do it. I would work for minimum wage if I had to.

"There's no rent to pay. This house is all paid for," she said, yawned, and jumped back into bed.

"Seriously? You're only eighteen. I don't get it."

"My aunt owned it; I used to live with her," she said, seemingly uninterested.

"She left?" I asked.

"You could say that."

This was another untouchable subject, so I left it alone and lay down beside her. It was Monday, and yes, I should have been at school. But I wasn't, and I didn't care. Sam rolled into my arms and rested her head against my shoulder. We lay together for hours, falling in and out of sleep, discussing typical favorites such as foods, colors, hairstyles, music, games, words, and of course, animals.

By the time supper came around, it was as though I'd known Sam for years, and I'm certain she felt the same way. I'd never felt so connected to another human being before—I don't think I could ever truly describe it if I wanted to. Being with Matt, my ex, had never been like this. Sure, we had spent hours chatting side by side, but we never really got to *know* each other. I cared about what Sam thought. I observed her every facial expression to better understand her. I wanted to know what she was thinking about, when she was thinking about it, and how it made her feel. With Matt, it had always been so simple—he was either angry, happy, horny, or sad. With Sam, everything was hidden somewhere much deeper, and I was determined to find my way there.

"You want Chinese food tonight?" she whispered in my ear.

That sounded delicious, of course.

"Sounds great," I said and kissed her thick, pink lips.

I didn't return to school Tuesday morning. I can't quite explain what came over me, but nothing seemed to matter anymore. I felt so liberated—so capable of anything I wanted. I could eat whenever I wanted, whatever I wanted, and however often I wanted. Television viewing was endless, and Sam's body heat supplied my happiness. I had no responsibilities, and I possessed the freedom to do whatever I wished.

By the time Saturday came around (I hadn't realized it was Saturday until Sam pointed it out), fun took on a whole new meaning.

"You ever been down to the gay village?" Sam asked, flipping her cell phone open.

"Um, well I've been there. Who hasn't?" I asked.

I had walked through the large street a few times with my parents, but only because we were shopping in that area. My mother, quite frankly, had done everything in her power to limit her time spent crossing the village. A dirty, sinful place, she had called it.

"No, I mean in the clubs," Sam said.

I laughed at what I thought was a ridiculous question. Of course I hadn't been; I was only eighteen. Had I wished to go clubbing, I could have gone to Montreal, where eighteen was the legal age. But in Loshano, I had one more year to go before being entitled to absolute freedom.

"Why's that funny?" she asked.

"I'm not of age. Sorry, I thought you knew that."

"So?"

So? All right, so Sam had another trick up her sleeve, and I was dying to hear about it. I felt my lips stretch across my face. I knew that she was about to lure me into a new world.

"I'm not of age either, Kaity. It's called a fake ID. Don't tell me you've..." and she stopped, looked down at my beer, and smiled. "I forgot you were a sin virgin." I shrugged and nodded.

This wasn't offensive; it was the truth. I was, in fact, a sin virgin. A more factual term for this would have been a fun virgin. I had only picked up drinking last week, I had never had sex in my life, and no, I had never set foot in a club—straight or gay.

"Let's deflower you tonight," she said, grinning mischievously.

"Yeah, but I don't have a..." I said.

"Shush. Laura has a bunch. I'll hook you up," she said.

"Laura?"

"A friend. She's going to Taylor's Tower tonight, and we're going with her."

"Taylor's Tower?" I said.

"A club. A gay club. A lesbian club, to be more precise. It's great. You'll love it."

A gay club? Seriously? I wondered whether it would be weird or just downright fantastic.

"Drink up; you'll need it," she said and tilted my beer towards my face.

I was in shock—absolute shock—and excited of course.

"Don't worry. You'll love it. But I better not catch you talking too long with any other girl. You're a hot one, Kaity, and you're fresh meat."

"What? Fresh...?" I deflected the hot comment, which caused my cheeks to glow a light shade of pink. She thought I was hot? I beamed.

She laughed. "I'll keep an eye on you."

By nine o'clock, Sam had dressed us up and fixed our makeup. She looked incredible. I had a hard time focusing on myself. All I wanted to do was grope her. She wore tight, black jeans, and a pink V-cut top. She had a thick, silver chain around her neck, many black bracelets, thick eyeliner, black nail polish, and well, her perfect, curvy body. What a goddess, I thought, staring at her as she modeled her way into the room. I sipped on my sixth beer and swallowed hard.

She forced me to let my hair loose, which hung down my back and around my shoulders. Although usually dark, it looked much lighter in comparison to hers. And even though I was slightly shorter, her gray jeans and yellow top fit me quite nicely. They were snug but very comfortable.

Her crystal-like eyes scanned me from top to bottom, narrowing as they went.

"I might have to keep a leash on you," she said, smirking.

My knees buckled. *Please do*, I thought.

"Shut up," I said and threw a sofa cushion her way.

I heard something vibrate, and she ran to find her phone.

"Hello? Yeah. Yeah, for sure. Ya, okay. See you soon," and she hung up. "They're meeting us near the patio outside of the Tower. We'll pick a floor after."

"A floor? How many floors are there?" I asked.

"Seven," she said, her tone nonchalant.

"What? Seven? That's insane! Sounds like a mini hotel." I realized immediately how airheaded that must have sounded. Mini hotel? What was wrong with me? Fortunately, she ignored my hotel comment.

"You like vodka?" she asked.

"Um. Wouldn't know," I said.

"Come here; you're doing a shot, and then we're leaving."

I loved being bossed around by her—being told what to do without first being asked how I felt about it. She was a queen in my eyes, and I was willing to bow down to her—to obey her every command.

I followed her into the kitchen, and she poured me a clear shot of Stolichnaya. I didn't bother smelling it, because I didn't want to look weak. I mimicked her action and quickly poured it down my throat. Holy burn! I felt the strong fluid attempt its way back up into my throat and out of my mouth.

"Chase it!" Sam said, pressing my beer bottle against my lips.

I did exactly that and swore to myself that I would never again do a vodka shot (empty promise, of course, because I have grown to love vodka). Sam arranged for a cab to drive us downtown and also paid for the ride. I felt guilty because I had no money. I wanted to contribute, but I couldn't. This would change. I would get a job.

The view downtown was much more colorful than I remembered it to be. There were bright lights everywhere—blue, yellow, red, orange, green. It was remarkable. I knew we had arrived at the gay village the minute we were there. Everywhere I turned, same-sex couples walked together, holding hands.

Who knew Loshano had so many gays? This was spectacular! Sam hugged me around the neck as if to say, "It's great, isn't it?"

I wondered how often she came down here. And if it was often, why was she still single? Sam was beyond gorgeous and so much fun.

"Laura!" Sam called out, waving to two girls standing by a patio.

It was chilly outside, seeing as we were now in October, so I was surprised to see the number of smokers chatting outside, sipping their drinks around empty chairs.

"Hey lady, how's it going?" the blonde girl said, leaning in to hug Sam. "Wow, who's your friend?" she asked, looking at me with her round, blue eyes.

"Back off bitch, she's mine," Sam joked.

I shook Laura's hand and introduced myself.

She was very sporty looking with a muscular jawline and blonde hair tied back in a tight ponytail. I was introduced to Joelle, or Jo, who was probably the most boyish of us all. She had short, spiky brown hair, a baggy T-shirt, and sagging jeans. To be quite honest, this was the image I had initially associated with that of a lesbian, before being pulled out of my ignorance. It was what I always saw on TV—masculine butches. But as I looked around, I was beginning to understand that lesbians, just as straight girls, came in many different shapes and sizes. This was a new reality for me.

"Here," Laura said, handing me a driver's license.

"What's this?" I asked, looking down. It was some girl I had never seen before, but she did resemble me quite a bit.

"I have a stack of them. Brunettes, blondes, redheads, you name it," Laura said and winked.

Sam grabbed Laura by the face and kissed her cheek.

"You're a lifesaver, babe," she said and grabbed my hand to lead me into the club.

So that night, I was twenty-three years old. Was I scared when the bouncer asked for my ID? Hell yes. I was terrified, but the alcohol in my system aided me in maintaining a cool attitude.

Unbelievable! That's all I could think. The

place was jam-packed with all sorts of people. I nearly choked when I saw a seven-foot woman walk by me with her perfect, muscular body. I later found out that this had been a man. I was in awe.

"You're cute," Sam said. She educated me about drag queens, transgendered people, lipstick lesbians, butches, femmes, and versatile lesbians.

"The key," she said, "is to look first at the chest and then for an Adam's apple."

I eventually got the hang of it, although it was difficult at first. I was most surprised to see tall women with heels, skirts, and tiny purses (lipstick lesbians, as Sam taught me). Never would I have visualized a lesbian who could look so, well, feminine, which was rather hypocritical of me, since I wasn't exactly a butch myself.

Sam went around hugging different girls here and there, which proved that she was a regular here. I somehow felt proud to be the one she had fallen for. I could only hope she wasn't a player. The thought frightened me, so I pushed it away. As the night went on, I must have met well over twenty people, whose names I would never remember. I do remember, however, dancing with an attractive lipstick lesbian. Sam had been quick to intervene and pull me away. She was so territorial, and I loved it.

Around two a.m., we stumbled our way out of Taylor's Tower and walked down the village street, alongside different dance clubs and a few dominatrix bars.

"Let's get poutine. I'm starving," Sam said. She led me to a tiny, family-owned restaurant at the corner of the street.

Only then did I notice that Laura and Jo were nowhere to be seen. I wasn't even sure when we had separated, but I was now with Sam, and that was all that mattered. She ordered us a large poutine with two forks. It was the most amazing late-night meal I ever had. We laughed as the melted cheese curds dripped from the corners of our mouths, and the fat, gravy-coated fries fell all over the table. But the fun ended rather abruptly.

"Hey girls," came some guy's voice.

I looked over to the table beside us and saw three young jocks, smiling suggestively our way.

Sam rolled her eyes and shook her head at me as if to say, "Ignore them."

"Aw, come on. Don't be like that," said the shortest of them all.

He stood up, walked over, and sat down beside Sam. My heart started pounding. I wasn't used to this. Would they not leave us alone? Were they dangerous? Or were they just horny, drunken boys?

"I'm on a date. Please leave me alone," Sam said coldly, not once glancing his way.

She stared at her food, her knuckles whitening as she clenched her fork.

"On a date? With who?" the guy asked, a cocky grin on his face. He looked around, and then laughed with his friends, who were still seated at their table.

Sam dropped her fork and stared at him, her mouth partially filled with french fries. She spat out her food and clenched her jaw.

"With my beautiful girlfriend," she said, extending an open palm my way.

The guy looked at me. To be honest, all I had heard was *girlfriend*. Girlfriend. Sam's girlfriend. Was this drunk talk? Or had she meant it?

"This sexy thing? We've got some girl-on-girl action, boys," the guy said, turning to his friends.

The other two laughed but didn't come to our table.

"Leave them alone, man," one of them said.

"Come on Kaity, we're done here," Sam said. "Move," she ordered, sliding against the seated dumbass.

He did as told and stood up. Sam grabbed my hand and quickly led me out of the restaurant.

"Sorry about that, Kaity," she said, walking rapidly.

"Come on, man, wait up," the guy said.

His friends followed him, and us, out of the restaurant. I was now beginning to worry. Why were they following us? The streets were much emptier than they had been earlier, which only intensified my fear. No one was around.

"Hey, I said wait," the guy repeated, and he squeezed his fingers around Sam's wrist.

"What the fuck, man?" Sam shouted. She swung her body around to face him and yanked her wrist out from his hand.

"Come on now, you're not telling me you're gay, are you?" he asked.

"That's exactly what I'm telling you. I asked you nicely to leave us alone, okay?" she said and turned away from him again.

But this hadn't pleased him. Again, he pulled on her with his large, muscular hand.

"Dude, fuck off," Sam snapped.

"Calm down, sweetheart. I'm only tryin' to help you out," he said. "You're way too hot to be a lesbian. I know what your real problem is. You haven't fucked the right man yet." He laughed and cupped his dick.

And I knew that things were about to get a whole lot worse when Sam lunged forward and shoved him hard. He stumbled back a few steps and nearly fell against his friends.

"I'd rather fuck your mother than lay a finger on you," Sam said and spat on his shoe.

He frowned and moved towards Sam, but she quickly swung a fist to the side of his face. Crack. It set him off. I couldn't believe what was happening. Within seconds, the guy was on top of Sam, and I could hear his fists bashing violently against her face. I screamed as loud as my lungs would allow and I jumped on his back. But he just shouldered me away and I fell to the ground. I heard a few more cracks before his friends tore him off, shouting things I couldn't understand.

"Fucking bitch!" the guy shouted.

His face was red, and he was breathing heavily. His friends pulled him back, telling him that everything was okay. I rushed to Sam's side and grabbed her by the face. Her right eye was entirely swollen and her bottom lip was fat and covered in blood.

"Fucking asshole," she muttered. She laughed, causing several droplets of blood to sprinkle on my shirt.

At that moment, had I been given a gun, I know I would have shot that guy square in the face. I wanted to kill him. But I was a thin, 5'5" girl with no muscle, no weapon, and no fighting experience. They were three young men. Even though I was drunk, my intelligence kicked in and told me to let it go. All I could do was thank

God that the smallest of them had been the one with a bad temper. Blows like that from a large man's fist could have severely damaged Sam's face, or worse, could have killed her. The guys were finally gone, and we were left in the dark, empty street. I hugged her close and cried and cried and cried.

I don't remember much after that, but I do remember a few biker guys from the dominatrix bar coming to help us find a cab.

Everything else was black to me.

Chapter 8

I licked my dry lips and cracked open my eyes. Day of the week: uncertain. Last night: gay club. Oh. This meant today was Sunday. I recollected the pieces, until my surroundings came into focus. What lay before me was wholly heartbreaking. Sam's face had swollen like a balloon, and she was smiling at me with one open eye. The other had been forced shut, due to the heavy blows she had received.

"Oh, Sam," I said and gently rested an open palm on her delicate neck.

"Hey," she said, "how do I look?"

"Probably just as you feel," I said.

"Fair enough. I'm sorry you had to see that," she said.

"Me too," I said. I wanted to cry again as I stared at her beaten face.

How could someone harm something so beautiful? I wanted to fix her, to erase all that had happened. She closed her good eye and inhaled a deep breath. Her lip twitched and her eyebrows nearly touched each other.

"She OD'd last year," she said.

I was about to speak but thought it best to be silent—to listen.

"My aunt. She overdosed on heroin in the living room. This house was hers."

Her one eye opened again, searching me.

"Sam, I'm..." I tried.

"It's okay, really. We weren't that close," she said.

"Still, I'm really..."

"You're the first person I've ever shared that with," she said.

I didn't know what to say or how to react. I brushed her black hair behind her ear and kissed her forehead. This must have been all she wanted. She smiled and grabbed my hand. We didn't speak after that. I fell back into a world of drunken dreams, only to awaken once the sun had descended.

"Morning, sunshine."

I looked up at Sam's multicolored face and grimaced.

"Don't look at me like that," she said.

"I'm sorry. I hate seeing you that way." I reached for her hand.

"It'll pass; don't worry." Instead of grabbing my hand, she lit up and offered me a plate of what appeared to be macaroni and cheese.

"Where'd you get this?" I asked, beaming at her.

"I made it."

"I thought you didn't cook," I said.

"I don't. But I guess I'm going to have to learn if I want to feed you properly," she said.

I looked down at the plate again. The presentation was a mess. It looked like something that had been vomited right into the plate. But the excitement in her one good eye, combined with the fact that she had tried so hard to cook me a meal, weakened me. I watched her lip curl up in a shy manner I'd rarely seen before. It was as if she was a puppy awaiting praise for a good trick. She was the most fascinating person I had ever met, and I knew that I had fallen in love.

"Well?" she asked, looking up at me.

She looked so pathetic, so cute. I gave her the biggest smile my lips would allow, sat up, and grabbed the plate. She watched in anticipation as I took a bite. It wasn't all that bad. It wasn't the best, but knowing that her hands had created it made it the best meal I had ever eaten.

"This is really good," I said, half honestly.

"Yeah? You like?" she asked.

"Yeah, I love you." That was not at all what I had intended to say. My heart sank and I quickly glanced up at her. Maybe she hadn't heard it.

"What?" she asked, taken aback.

"I said I love it," I corrected myself, smiling stupidly.

She grinned and jumped back into bed with me. As I finished my meal, I wondered if she had truly heard what I said, but had ignored it, and if she had heard it, whether or not she felt the same, but was too afraid to admit it. Probably not—I had known her for what, a few weeks? I didn't understand how I could feel so intensely about another person so soon. It didn't make any sense. I placed my plate on the bedside table and turned to face her. She still had that goofy smile on her face, that proud look of successful accomplishment. Adorable. I laid my head on her shoulder and wrapped an arm over her stomach.

"Kaity?" she asked.

"Yeah?" I said.

"Have you talked to your parents since, well, you know?"

I sat upright and looked back at her. I'm uncertain why I thought this humorous, but I started laughing.

"Why's that funny?" she asked.

"I don't know. I completely forgot about them."

I couldn't believe it. All of my time spent

with Sam had caused me to forget everything: school, Amy and Andrew, my mom, my dad, Matt, and the fact that I'd basically been kicked out of my own home. I had spent the whole week hiding here, utterly carefree.

"Aren't you going back to school?" I finally asked.

"Why bother?" she said. "I make great money doing nothing. I don't see what could be any better than that."

"Don't you want a better future?" I asked.

"Kaity, relax. We're young. Now's the time to enjoy life." She grabbed the back of my shirt and pulled me in close to her. "Take the year off and go back next year," she added.

I nearly scolded her for having even suggested such a ridiculous idea, but some part of me started to think that maybe this wasn't such a bad idea. I was having so much fun here. What harm could one year off possibly cause? Besides, there were alternate programs for dropout students, which, inexplicably, took far less time to complete than all of high school itself.

What was I doing? I felt a rush of happiness surge through me—a sense of danger, of adventure that I couldn't quite explain. I was being rebellious, and I loved it. This was so unlike me.

"So?" she asked.

"Why not?" I said and I hugged her tight.

"Yeah! Fuck it, right?"

"Fuck it," I agreed, and tenderly kissed her swollen lips.

She kissed me back, again and again. And before I knew it, her hand was sliding up my shirt and sneaking its way into my bra. I didn't stop her. I wanted this. I wanted this more than anything. I kept my eyes closed and allowed her to rub my breasts, my stomach, and my thighs. My breathing grew heavy when her lips began to caress my lower stomach and then my inner thighs. She delicately unbuttoned my jeans and slid them down along with my panties, leaving me bare and vulnerable to her hot breath. Her warm tongue slid across my inner leg, teasing me. I dug my fingernails into her arms and arched my back as she made me feel something I never knew was possible.

Chapter 9

After I finished my shower and made my way into Sam's room for a change of clothes, I spotted my cell phone lying on the floor at the foot of her bed. I picked it up and flipped it open—it was dead. I wondered if Matt had tried texting or calling me, or if anyone else from school—whose numbers I only had for convenience—had attempted to contact me to see whether or not I was still alive. The truth was, I didn't care. I was in no hurry to purchase a cell phone charger or to call my parents. For all they knew, I was dead. I wondered if they even cared. Surely, this was pessimistic thinking. Of course, they cared. I was still their daughter, after all.

These thoughts soon led me to feel guilty. I found myself wanting to call my mother. So I borrowed Sam's cell phone and dialed home. Fortunately, the answering machine picked up;

I left a message:

"Hey, Mom, Dad, it's me. I wanted to let you know that I'm safe, alive... Oh, and my cell phone's dead. So, I don't know, I'll call you again sometime. Love you, bye." I hung up, realizing I had been a bitch for not having called them sooner, but hey, I had honestly forgotten. I was busy now.

I dried my hair, threw on some of Sam's clothes, and made my way to the living room. As I walked down the hallway, I was taken aback by Laura's presence.

"Hey, girl," she said, walking right past me.

"Hey," I managed to let out, and I watched her enter the bathroom. Sam was sitting on the sofa as usual, but with Travis by her side.

"Hey, Kaity! Come try this. Travis just picked it up," Sam said.

"Try what?" I asked, but I knew she was referring to the lit smoke in her hand.

And I also knew that it wasn't a cigarette because of its potent smell. She stretched it out and nodded as if to draw me in. I had never tried weed before and didn't much care to. It was one thing to drink, but to get into drugs?

She must have read my thoughts; smiling, she closed her eyes.

"Weed doesn't count as a drug, Kaity. Relax. Come on," she said, wiggling the little stick between her thumb and index finger. "It's outdoor blueberry kush. It's amazing."

Outdoor? What did that mean? And was I really about to smoke marijuana? D.A.R.E. suddenly popped into my mind—the program's clear warnings to steer away from peer pressure, to avoid drugs at all costs. All of this education, and yet I had no desire to use it. I gave in and sat beside her. The smell was strong, but I knew I'd get used to it.

Travis was cutting up the green stuff and rolling it into a very thin-looking paper. He must have noticed me staring, because he looked back at me, smiled, and said, "What? Am I doing a bad job?"

I didn't have time to respond.

"Kaity's never smoked, Travis. Give her a break," Sam said. She handed me a lit joint. "You have to inhale it into your lungs, and then hold your breath. Don't suck in too much, otherwise, it'll burn and you'll cough like crazy. Got it?"

I nodded with uncertainty and pinched the tiny stub out of her fingers. My first few attempts were weak because I feared the burning sensation.

"Come on," Sam pressed.

I sucked in harder, and although it was better than my first attempts, I overdid it. I did feel the burn: the nasty burn that spread down my throat and into my lungs. A huge cloud of white came blasting out of my pipes and around my eyes, and I coughed uncontrollably.

"Too much, babe, too much," I heard Sam say over my loud, self-induced barking.

Travis laughed, but he remained focused on his task. Sam took the joint back and continued to puff on it as I leaned over, head in between my legs. I didn't like weed. As I squeezed my watery eyes shut and wiped the drool from my lips, I promised myself that I would never touch weed again. But of course, five minutes later, I was at it again. I wasn't very good at holding onto my own promises. I felt spacey, light-headed. I looked down at my hands to assure myself that they were still intact. I could barely feel them anymore. I was going numb. Was this normal?

"Kaity, chill. Stop breathing so hard," Sam said. "You're gonna feel funny at first, but you'll learn to like it." Her eyes were bloodshot.

My eyelids became heavy as if I hadn't slept in days.

"Oh," was all I said, and I burst out laughing.

Sam too, chuckled with me for a while, and by the end of it, I had completely forgotten what it was we were laughing about. I suddenly noticed Laura emerging from the hallway and walking towards us. She rubbed her pink nose several times with the back of her hand and sat on the recliner chair across from the sofa.

"Sup?" she asked. She crossed her legs and

looked away, her eyes considerably wide for no apparent reason.

"Dude, I thought I still had my stash, but I'm all out. Can it wait till Thursday?" Travis asked, gazing up worriedly at Laura.

"What the fuck? I just took my last line," Laura said, her eyes wider now, resembling the size of golf balls.

"Look, I'm sorry. I'll do what I can," Travis said. He shook his matted blond hair to one side, away from his eyes, and stared at her, waiting for compliance.

"Whatever, man. I'll get it somewhere else; it's all good." She shrugged and leaned back into her chair.

"Hey Kaity, how's it going?" she asked, pointing her chin at me.

"Good," I said. I looked at Sam and burst into another laughing fit.

This feeling wasn't bad—not bad at all. I had thought alcohol was a substance to relieve me of my worries, but this, this was no doubt an "I don't give a shit about anything right now" kind of sensation. A high, Sam had explained.

"Sam, you wanna see Chris and Jordan at lunch?" Laura asked.

"I don't think Kaity's really into that stuff, sorry," Sam said, glancing sideways in my direction.

"I didn't ask you if Kaity wanted to go. It's

you and me, man," Laura said, "for old times' sake."

"Kaity goes where I go," Sam said. The humor in her eyes was suddenly gone.

"Since when? What, has this chick got you whipped?" Laura asked.

She was getting so defensive. What did she care? Weren't they just friends?

"Shut the fuck up, man," Sam said.

She flicked her joint onto the living room carpet and disappeared into the kitchen. She was back with two beers, and I could tell that she was still angered by Laura's comment.

"Come on, Sam. Me and you," Laura said.

"I said no, okay?" Sam said. "Fuck," and she cracked open the beers.

"I don't know who this Kaitlyn is, but she's sucked all the fun right out of you," Laura said.

I was uncomfortable at this point. Although neither one of them looked at me, I felt attacked. Was I really changing Sam for the worse?

"Laura, you're fucking amped. Get out of my house, and come back later," Sam said, slamming her beer bottle onto the coffee table.

"I'm not going anywhere. Don't treat me like some friend, Sam. I've known you for how long now?"

"I don't give a shit. You're being a bitch. Get out," Sam said.

"Girls, girls, stop it. I'm trying to focus here," Travis said calmly, still chopping away at his huge pile of weed.

"Shut up, Travis!" Laura snapped and looked back at Sam.

This had been a mistake. I had never seen Travis upset before. He was always so calm. But I now knew that he had a backbone.

"All right, that's it," Travis said. "Laura, get out. Right now."

He walked briskly towards Laura and grabbed her by the arm.

"Don't fucking touch me!" She swung away from him and shot him the nastiest look possible.

"I said get out!" he shouted, his face reddening a darker shade with every word.

He was much taller than all of us, and I was thankful to have a male present right then. Had it been only Sam and me, things could have gotten very ugly, very fast.

Realizing that she was outnumbered, Laura snatched her jacket from the closet and stormed out. *What was up her ass?* I nearly asked, but I refrained from doing so. All would be explained to me when the time was appropriate. Sam drank her beer and stared at the table, obviously still upset by what had happened. When she finally noticed that I was watching her, she forced a smile, affectionately squeezed the back of my neck, and said, "Sorry about that."

"It's okay." But I couldn't keep quiet, as hard as I tried to. "Was she your…?" I asked.

"Ew, Kaity, no. We've never dated," she laughed, "she has jealousy issues, and she's always high on something, so that doesn't help."

"Who are Chris and Jordan?" I asked.

Had this been too much? Was I pushing it? She stirred uncomfortably in her seat and looked at Travis.

"I get it. Girl talk. I'm out of here," he said, flaunting a gorgeous set of whites.

The moment he left, Sam gently rubbed her fingers along the soft hairs of my arm and looked up at me with a worried, frightened look.

"What is it?" I pressed.

"Promise you won't think less of me?" she asked.

"I promise," and I meant it, of course.

"Chris and Jordan are these two drug dealers at St. George's High School. They trade coke, for, well, sex."

A knot formed in my throat. Please, no. Please.

"Kaity, not me," Sam said quickly.

I exhaled a breath of relief and tried to calm my heart.

"I was her lookout. She'd do them both in

the forest to get a couple days' worth of blow," she said.

I bit my lip and stared at her, now understanding why she hadn't wanted to take me there. Prostitution was not something I would have felt comfortable with. The more I learned about Sam, the more I realized how little I knew about her. There were so many stories—so many past experiences she had suffered through.

"Yeah," she said awkwardly, "so have you talked to your parents?"

It had been nearly two weeks since I had spoken to my mother.

"No," I said blankly.

"Maybe you should try again," she said.

This wasn't what I had expected to hear. I had expected that wild, carefree attitude she consistently projected.

"Why do you care? I don't see you calling your parents."

My stomach sank the second I said it. Maybe it was a warning from my subconscious, from common sense itself. Or maybe it was the way her eyes changed shape and narrowed at me. I had crossed the line. How far, I wasn't yet certain.

"You can be a real bitch sometimes, you know that?" She stood up and left.

I wasn't sure whether to be angrier at the

bitch comment or at myself for having opened my big mouth. She hadn't wanted to speak about her parents since the day I met her, and I had just attacked that precise area of her life. I didn't chase her. I simply sat still, staring at the living room's filthy, brown carpet. I heard her bedroom door slam shut and I flinched. How could I be such a moron? I never imagined being on Sam's bad side. I had seen her get angry before, but never with me.

Eventually, I took a few deep breaths, swallowed my fear, and made my way to her room. She was lying on her bed when I entered, facing the wall.

"Sam?" I said, trying to sound as innocent as possible.

"Get out," she ordered.

"Sam, I'm..."

"Get. Out. Now." Her tone was ice cold.

I almost fell apart at the harsh sound of her words. I wanted nothing more than to lie against her, to hold her. I hated this feeling. I was so powerless. Not knowing what else to do, I did the only thing I had been taught to—I made my way into the kitchen and pulled a beer out of the fridge.

I'm not sure when, where, or how I woke up, but I did. My eyes barely opened due to dehydration, and I grabbed the nearest liquid I could find—more beer.

"You proud of yourself?" Sam asked.

I looked up at her. She was leaning against the dining room wall, and the light behind her head forced my eyes shut again. I suddenly heard footsteps and loud clinging around me, so I reopened my eyes. Sam was cleaning what must have been well over ten beer bottles. She didn't speak.

I looked around some more. I realized that I had passed out on the floor, partially covered by the living room table.

"Here," Sam said, handing me a bottle of water. She sat down behind me on the sofa.

I lazily dropped back to the ground and pressed my fingers against my pulsating temples.

"Getting drunk doesn't fix anything, Kaity," Sam said coldly.

"You're one to talk," I said.

Gah! What was wrong with me? I couldn't believe those words had just come out of my mouth. My filter was gone! Although I should have been nervous, I wasn't. I felt so numb. I was still drunk.

"Fuck you," Sam said.

"Right back at you."

What was I doing? Why was I being so unlike me? This wasn't me. I was caring and loving. I wasn't a heartless bitch. But all I wanted to do was fight. I was angry. Angry at myself, angry at the world, angry at my parents, and somehow, this hatred had all managed to be misdirected at Sam.

"Pack your shit and go home," Sam said.

Chapter 10

I didn't have the strength or the courage to defend myself. My mother hugged me tight when I arrived on her doorstep, dirty and hungover. She didn't release me for what felt like hours, and I stood there with both arms dangling at my sides, refusing to reciprocate the hug.

"Where were you? Are you okay? Oh my goodness, Kaity, you look so sick. What have you done? Are you okay?" she ranted.

I shrugged and walked past her, up to my room.

"Kaity!" she called out behind me, but I didn't yell back.

I ignored her, as I did Amy when she said hi. When I entered my room, I threw my dead phone to the floor and fell into bed. I was out within seconds.

KNOCK, KNOCK.

I moaned and rolled over. Maybe Sam had come to apologize, to feed me some homemade macaroni and cheese. When I opened my eyes, I realized that I was no longer at Sam's, and everything fell into its awful place again. She had kicked me out. I was now home, unwanted by my own family, out of school, and jobless: the perfect recipe for a depression soufflé.

"Kaity?" I heard my dad say. He slowly creaked the door open and walked in. "Come on. We let you sleep for hours. You can't possibly still be tired."

"Hey, Dad," I said, my back facing him. I felt a weight press down at the corner of my bed, but I still didn't move.

"Where have you been all this time? You had us worried sick," he said.

"A friend's place."

"You been holding up all right?" he asked.

"Yeah."

"Look, your mother and I are very sorry about how things ended with us. We want to make it better, but you have to give us a chance, okay? This is hard on us, too," he said.

Oh, was it? Was it really that hard on them? What the hell did they care? They weren't the ones who would be forced to spend a life most likely alone, constantly defending who they were as a person. I was the one suffering, here. I wouldn't have a kind, rich boyfriend to support me. I wouldn't have a wedding with both sides of the family genuinely happy and accepting of my decision. No, I was the one who was destined to live a life fighting off bullshit. And this speech, this speech of his right now, was just the beginning of the bullshit I'd have to put up with. I suddenly remembered Sam's beaten face, and nearly broke down. But I swallowed it back. I had to be strong.

"Look, Kaity. We know you dropped out of school, and that's your decision. But if you want to live here, we can't have you moping around all day. You need to get yourself a job. We won't force you to go to church, but there won't be any girls sleeping here," he said.

He walked out. He had cut right to the point: no sympathy, no love, no understanding. It was their way or the highway. And, well, I couldn't afford the highway—I couldn't even afford a bus pass. I would simply have to comply.

I didn't speak much to my family for the remainder of the week. I spent most of my days lying in bed, suffering from cold sweats and the shakes. This, I assumed, was heartbreak. But, as I now know, it most definitely was not. If only heartbreak were so brief—so simple. Alcohol withdrawal was my problem. I considered buying my own alcohol a few times to relieve myself of the symptoms, but Laura had taken back the fake ID. Instead, I suffered through it with only one thought on my mind—Sam. How had things gone from being so wonderful to so terrible? I hated my life.

Every day, I considered trying to call Sam, or at the very least, to text her. I wanted to speak to her more than anything, but every time the urge came about, a few facts popped into my head:

If Sam truly cared about me, she would have called me by now. She was the chaser, the dominant one. It was her job to come to me.

If, let's say, she did answer my phone call, I risked the chance of being told to piss off—to never call her again. And this would only hurt some more.

She kicked ME out, knowing perfectly well that I had no place to go (neither happily nor unconditionally).

I lay in bed that night, wondering if Sam had faked every part about liking me. Was I in love with someone who didn't give a damn about me? Was I even in love? I tried my best to deny my feelings, but no matter how angry or hurt I was, I wished her no harm. I still wanted to kiss her delicate face, no matter how rigid its features were. And it still killed me to see her beaten, swollen face in my mind, and how stern she had looked when she told me to leave. I drove myself crazy with assumptions—false hopes. Perhaps she had lost my phone number? That was reason enough to call her, wasn't it? No, she hadn't lost it. Maybe she had lost her phone, I thought. No one remembers numbers by heart anymore, what with technology and all. *Stop it, just stop it.*

I wiped a few tears out of my eyes and blinked repeatedly. I missed her so much. Why the hell wasn't she calling me!?

FUCK!

I punched my mattress and molded my face into the curve of my pillow, before bursting into an irrepressible crying fit.

Chapter 11

My eyes were swollen when I woke up to the sound of knocking at my door. Supper was ready, yet again, and I rushed to the bathroom to fix my face. A little powder here, a little concealer there, and I was good to go. I walked down to what I expected would be my family, and only my family. But to my surprise, Andrew was seated beside Amy. Great. Romance being shoved right in my face. I nearly turned around, but I realized it would have been rude. So, I forced my feet to make their way to the dining room and I lazily dropped into my chair.

Roast beef, mashed potatoes, and steamed vegetables. Although I knew that the food looked delicious, I didn't have the slightest urge to eat anything. I hadn't eaten all day, nor had I eaten yesterday, but I wasn't hungry. On the bright side, my lack of appetite was helping me lose the weight I had gained eating takeout and drinking beer with Sam (ten pounds, to be exact).

I stared at the potatoes. As I picked at my food, not caring about the conversations my family and their new replacement of me (Andrew) were currently having, my attention shifted outward when I heard my name.

"Hello?" Amy asked, widening her eyes at me.

"Huh?" I mumbled.

"Didn't you hear anything I just said?" she asked.

"Sorry, I was zoning out," I said.

"Andrew can get you a job!" she said, flashing her set of bright whites at Andrew, more so than at me.

"There you go. That's what you need," my dad said.

"Oh," I said. I hadn't noticed my tone of carelessness until Amy wrinkled her nose and furrowed her eyebrows.

"Oh?" she repeated.

"I mean, where?" I asked.

"That little pharmacy on Joseph Street... You know, the um...?"

"Lacey's Pharmacy," Andrew said, smiling lovingly her way.

Ugh.

"Right! Lacey's! Well, his cousin's the owner. You can start next Monday. It's all been set up!"

Amy said.

I stared at her for a moment. Was I supposed to thank her? Was this a good thing? Did I want to work? All I wanted to do was dig myself into a hole and bury dirt over my head. Then again, work would probably help keep my mind occupied.

"Really?" It was all I could say.

I looked at Andrew, nodded modestly, and then at my parents. They both seemed to think that this was the best thing for me. I took a bite of my potatoes, looked up at Amy's expectant eyes, and forced a smile.

"That's great," I said.

"I know, and it's all thanks to Andrew. We had no idea you were looking for a job. I mean, I don't know what you've been up to the past couple of weeks, so, you know..." She looked at my mom and paused. "Well anyways, Andrew says you'll have a lot of fun there. The employees are nice."

I finished my supper, thanked my family, and returned to my room. A new job? Would this be a good thing? I didn't want to work. I wanted to sleep my life away. I wanted to rot here, in my bed, all alone. But on the other hand, working would aid me in forgetting my current situation. Distraction was key.

BEED-A-LEEP.

Speaking of distraction. I quickly unplugged

my cell phone from its charger on my dresser and held it close to my chest. *Please be Sam. Please be Sam. Please, please, please!* All right, enough! I took a deep breath and forced myself to have *no expectations.* It probably wasn't even from her, anyways. It couldn't be. Or maybe... *Stop it!* No *expectations.* I slowly opened it up, as if speed had any effect on the message's sender, and exhaled a sigh of defeat when my true hopes were crushed. The message was from Matt:

"U ignorin my calls now?"

Great. Well, I guess this meant he had tried calling me a few times when I had been with Sam. I pressed *reply* and rubbed my thumb against the shiny keys. What would I say? But then it dawned on me that I wasn't attached to a leash. I wasn't his. I didn't belong to anyone. If I didn't want to communicate with the outside world, then I wouldn't communicate. I closed my phone and chucked it on the floor in a rebellious manner, but not too far as to deny my future reach—I would check it again in an hour.

I lay there, painfully pondering every aspect of my current situation. I was going to begin work in a week. I had not completed high school. For a moment, I considered returning to school. It wasn't too late. A few detentions, perhaps a suspension for my absences, and a whole lot of homework would be the result of my two-week party, but really—what was the point?

Return to school for what? To sit there, day in, day out, wondering if Sam would come back to fill the empty seat beside me? She wasn't going back. And neither was I. The thought of socializing with my classmates caused a throbbing pain in my temples. Work was also going to involve socializing, but at least with strangers. I would forget my old life to begin a new one. There was no other way.

I closed my eyes and tried to erase Sam's face. It worked, for a few seconds. The image of Amy and Andrew occasionally popped into my head, and then other TV romances made their appearances. Any thought of love or dating caused a huge lump to climb into the back of my throat. There was no winning—love was everywhere. I hated feeling this way. I missed her more than anything. How long was the pain supposed to last?

And although slightly obsessive, as the days went by, I routinely checked my cell phone to see if she had called. And by routinely, I mean hourly. I wanted her back. Why wasn't she calling me? The only thought that kept me from wanting to die in my sleep was that she would return to me soon, that she simply needed her space to cool off. My thoughts intertwined and everything lost meaning.

I woke up around midnight with drool on my face. How had I fallen asleep for so long? I jumped out of bed and of course, checked my phone. Nothing. Nothing! It had now been a week since our last contact, and I was beginning to worry. How long did she need to cool off? I threw a pillow over my head and wept myself back to sleep.

Three a.m. came around and I woke up again. I tossed and turned for nearly an hour before I finally kicked the blankets into the air and grabbed my phone. No messages yet again.

Really?

That was it! I couldn't take it anymore! I had to hear her voice. I knew I was being ridiculous when I blocked my number and dialed hers, but I didn't care. I needed to do it. Although it was four in the morning, chances were she'd be awake. I hit *call* and held the phone close to my ear. My heart was pounding.

"The number you are calling is unavailable at the moment. Please try again later," came the woman's annoying, robotic voice.

What did this mean? Was her phone dead? Or had she lost it? Had she canceled her services? She didn't know where I lived. Maybe she was looking for me but didn't know how to contact me. I considered taking my parents' car to go see her, but the rational side of me said not to. Come on, really? If her phone was out of service, it would be because she had decided to get rid of her phone.

Because of me? Maybe. Probably. I hoped so, in a sick way. Anger meant care. But at the same time, this made things very difficult. Maybe her phone was broken, and she was unable to retrieve my phone number. *Stop it, Kaity.* This was no excuse. I suddenly realized that if she wanted to speak with me, there were many ways of getting a hold of my number.

She could have gone back to school and asked a classmate for my number.

A phone book? They still exist, you know. She knew my family name.

Demanding to receive copies of her call records from the cell phone company.

Okay, so I was being obsessive. But, truthfully, she didn't want to speak to me. That was that. I allowed anger to replace my sadness, which was much easier. Fine. If she didn't want to speak to me, then so be it. I didn't want to speak to her, either.

I fumed until I passed out. This outrageous roller coaster of emotions went on to last the remainder of my final week off. I spent my days sleeping, with the occasional break to eat supper every night. I didn't much care for breakfast or lunch. And by Friday, I had dropped back down to my regular weight. But I didn't care. I was so lethargic, so tired all the time. Looking back, that entire week had been one big blur of sleep and irregular emotions. I knew that my life was about to do a complete 180 degrees when Monday morning came around.

I stared at myself in the mirror, as I powdered my pale, sunken face. I threw on a bit of mascara, fixed my hair, and put on some decent clothes. I had forgotten how it felt to get ready. I had gotten used to moping around in pajama pants and old T-shirts all day.

For the first time in what felt like months, I smiled at my reflection. I looked good. It was eight-thirty, and Andrew would pick me up in fifteen minutes. I quickly poured a bowl of cereal down my throat and grabbed my coat. When I glanced out the kitchen window, I saw something that I hadn't at all expected to see—snow. How had I not realized it? There was a fresh coat lying gracefully over every lawn and along many tree branches. It was magnificent. This little moment of mine ended when Andrew's car pulled into the driveway. I rushed out, locked the door, and hopped into the Lancer.

"Nice ride," was all I could think of.

"Thanks. My old man gave it to me," he said, smiling proudly.

For a student, Andrew wasn't doing too

badly at all. This car looked brand new.

"Do you work when you're not in school?" I asked.

"Yeah, for my dad. He's a mechanic, runs his own business from home. So the car was a form of salary."

"No way, that's awesome," I said, and I meant it.

Andrew wasn't such a bad guy. I had never disliked him. I had disliked seeing romance. And I still did, but I would simply have to get over it.

"Monday's my only day off. Are you cool with busing to work tomorrow?" he asked, insecurely glancing my way.

"Oh, yeah, for sure," I said.

The number 9 bus passed by my house every half hour. I knew that busing wouldn't be a problem. I had a few loonies and toonies left in my sock drawer. That was one of the uppers to living in a big city—transportation was extremely easy. I watched which way he drove as we made our way to the pharmacy. It wasn't far at all—only a bus ride away.

"So, here we are," he said, parking in the lot.

He followed me inside, and I stood there awkwardly as he walked around the counter and into the staff room.

"Hey, hey!" I heard someone call out. "How's it going man?"

There was a bit of chitchat, and then a tall,

black-haired man walked out with Andrew by his side.

"You must be Kaity. I'm David," the tall man said.

He seemed to be in his mid-thirties and was notably polite. He reached out, shook my hand, and said, "Welcome."

"Thanks," I said.

"See you guys. Enjoy your first day, Kaity." Andrew bowed his head and walked out the front door.

"Come," David said.

He placed a gentle hand on my shoulder, as he gave me a tour of the pharmacy and explained in detail how he operated and what kind of shifts I would be expected to work.

My hours would be the typical nine to five—full-time. This was perfect. I would be busy, and I would be making money for the first time in my life. The salary started at ten dollars an hour, which was great in my book. I would be working alone at the front cash register, with another employee who would be in charge of the cosmetics and perfume area at the back cash register. I was introduced to the pharmacist, Akif. He was a Middle Eastern, middle-aged man who didn't speak much but knew pretty well all there was to know about medication.

The other cashier was slated to arrive

within minutes and would also be the one to train me on cash. David showed me where most of the important products were shelved and handed me a store map locating every purchasable item. This, he said, could be kept at the front cash register for future customer inquiries.

I looked up when the store's bells jingled, and in walked a young, blonde-haired woman with a backpack over one shoulder.

"Hey Dave," she said, dropped her bag by the register, and smiled at me. "You must be Kaity."

I smiled back, awkwardly as usual, and extended my hand.

"Yep, that's me," I said.

"I'm Maddison, you can call me Maddi." She smirked and looked back at David. "So, am I in charge of training?"

"You bet," he said, gave her a set of keys, and placed a warm hand on my shoulders. "Don't be shy, Maddi doesn't bite. She'll train you well. You guys behave. Oh, and Maddi, I left some Halloween decorations in the staff room if you want to fix things up a bit."

He winked, grabbed his jacket, and shook my hand again.

"See you soon, Kaity. Call me if you have any questions," he said.

Maddi smiled at me, her arms crossed.

"So," she said excitedly.

"So," I repeated.

"We can start training now, or we can have fun and decorate. It's up to you."

Decorate? I thought. I couldn't believe I had forgotten about Halloween. Next Wednesday would be Halloween, and I had utterly dismissed it. What was I going to do? Was I even going to celebrate? These thoughts were not important right now. What was important was the present moment. I had done enough torturous thinking over the last week—enough was enough.

I shrugged, smiled at her, and said, "Decorating sounds like fun."

"Woo!" She patted me on the shoulder and ran into the staff room, returning with a big box full of shiny black-and-orange items.

"Let's do this thang," she said.

I looked around and then back at her. She had a goofy look on her face. I felt comfortable, warm. I knew I would have fun working there.

Chapter 12

By noon, we had finished decorating, and Maddi showed me how to work the cash register. I watched as customers came through, and she showed me everything step by step. I didn't usually like being around people, but Maddi was entertaining. She was loud, energetic, and outgoing. She was the exact opposite of me, which was precisely why we clicked.

I learned a lot of work-related information during the remainder of my shift, and Andrew was back at five o'clock to pick me up. Although this may sound odd, or even untrue, I didn't want to leave. I wanted to stay at work. Why go home, to where I was unwanted? Where I was miserable? But, I knew I'd return the next day, which was all that mattered.

"Sleep well. You'll need your strength tomorrow!" Maddi said, waving good-bye as I walked out of Lacey's and hopped into Andrew's car.

"So, how was work?" Andrew asked.

"Great, actually," I said. "The people are nice."

"Yeah, I knew you'd like it." He put the car in gear and drove me back home.

I thanked him for the ride, as he followed me inside where he was greeted by Amy's open arms. I ignored the lovebirds and went upstairs. Only after I hopped onto my bed did I notice something unusual: I had spent eight hours of my day entirely unaware of Sam's existence. I hadn't once thought about her! My eyes shot down at my phone, and I hesitantly reached for it. No messages, of course. What was I thinking? Her phone was no longer working. I had to stop torturing myself.

I lay there and thought about Matt. I felt guilty for not having made any contact with him since that drunken night, but to speak to him meant returning to the life I was trying to forget. He was the only connection left. Everyone else from school was nothing more than an acquaintance to me—a classmate. This whole letting go of the past was much easier, considering I didn't really have any friends.

I decided that this would be it. I would not contact Matt again, nor would I keep my cell phone. I planned to purchase a pay-as-you-go phone after work to entirely eradicate my old self. I had a job now. I would just ask someone to lend me money.

I arrived at work the next day, red-nosed from the cold wind. The bus ride hadn't been all that bad. I walked in and found Maddi stocking the shelves.

"Hey!" she said and handed me a little bracelet with a key attached. "That's yours, for the cash register."

I thanked her and brushed the golden key along the tips of my fingers. My very own key. It meant responsibility.

The day went on as smoothly as I had imagined. Maddi and I spent most of it chatting about people, TV shows, boys (not that I had meant any of my comments, but I wasn't ready to come out to her), and of course future aspirations. And I did buy a pay-as-you-go phone that evening with money Maddi generously loaned me. I promised to pay her back the moment I received my first paycheck.

By the time Friday came around, I knew my station pretty well. Maddi declared her confidence in me and left me alone at the cash register, so she could operate her station in the back. I agreed and spent most of my time reading magazines, stocking shelves, and listening to music. This job was great. It felt nothing like work.

I went home, content, but also nervous about the fact that it was Friday and I had no plans. What was I going to do? Sit at home? Watch TV? Ordinarily, I would have gone out with Matt, or better yet, spent my night with Sam. But these were both out of the question. I threw on some pajamas and went downstairs after supper. To my surprise, Andrew was there, yet again.

"Wanna join?" Amy asked, passing me a large bowl of hot, buttery popcorn.

I poked my head into the living room to see my parents and Andrew sitting in front of the large, flat-screen TV. Why not, I thought. And as I sat comfortably in my favorite recliner chair, a bowl of popcorn in hand, I wondered if it was difficult for my family to accept me as a lesbian or if they were still in denial. It was as if nothing had ever happened, and I was uncertain whether or not this was a good thing. Instead of overanalyzing my circumstance, I enjoyed my food and the movie *Rush Hour* with my family. They were the only people who were still in my life, regardless of their discomfort.

By Sunday night, I was excited to return to work. It kept me grounded; it kept me sane, although, I somehow wished that I could share this excitement with Sam. I wished that she could be here to support me, to hug me, and to tell me that she was proud. I felt a strange mixture of happiness and depression kick in, and I didn't know whether to cry or to laugh, so I did both until I fell asleep.

Maddi was perky as always when I arrived at work the next day. It was a delightful feeling to see a smiling, familiar face. It warmed my heart to have someone enjoy my presence and to like me, regardless of my lack of verbal skills. I felt at home here.

"I'm going to get pizza at Gabriel's for lunch. Come with me. We'll close the place for a bit. No one will notice," she said, throwing an empty box into the big pile of cardboard she had just constructed. She stuck out her tongue and winked.

I accepted her offer graciously and impatiently waited for noon to arrive. I spent the first half of my day reading all about the new diets and scanning through paparazzi pictures of makeup-less celebrities. Maddi and I usually ate at different times, since only two of us were on duty. But at precisely 12:01, she came running around from behind the shelves with a piece of paper in her hand.

"Tadaaa!" she said, showing me the slip which read, "Be back in ten minutes."

Fortunately, the store was empty of customers. Akif already knew we would be gone temporarily, so Maddi rushed me out and stuck the note on the front doors before locking everything up. There was still a bit of slushy snow outside, but all in all, it was a nice day. We walked down the street to where Gabriel's Pizza House was located. The line was short, so we ordered plain pepperoni slices and hurried out.

Maddi was giggling at her mischievousness, having left the store unattended. But typically, our fun had to be ruined by a group of boys. I heard a few whistles before I turned around to see four young guys grinning at us and knocking elbows into one another others' ribs. Idiots, I thought.

My stomach clenched. Taylor's Tower: bright lights; blurred vision; poutine; the guys outside; Sam's beaten face. A savage urge to turn around and yell at them overcame me, but Maddi's hand took me by surprise, and all of my hatred dissipated only to be replaced by weakness.

She grabbed my hand, leaned in close, and said, "Pretend you're a lesbian, it's funny."

She kissed me on the cheek. I felt a shock radiate from my head, all the way down to my toes. No one had touched me since Sam. But I shrugged it off. It was only a joke.

"No fucking way!" I heard the guys yell, and then amused laughter resonated throughout the streets.

I forced a laugh as Maddi and I held hands

and walked away, but if I thought that my previous nausea had been unpleasant, I was in for a surprise. I nearly fell to my knees when I spotted a dark figure standing across the street at the bus stop, staring me cold in the eyes. My stomach sank. Her bright green eyes stared painfully my way, and then at my hand which was currently wrapped around Maddi's warm fingers.

"Shit!" was all I could say, and I tore my hand from Maddi's.

I hardly noticed Maddi's confusion, because I became too dizzy to concentrate on anything but Sam's eyes. I opened my mouth, as if about to shout something, then closed my eyes and bit my lower lip. What was I supposed to do? Run over there and talk to her? I wanted to tell her the truth. I wasn't *with* Maddi. She was straight! *Please, Sam, please understand*, was all I could think. *Please don't hate me.*

I saw her viciously chuck the remainder of her cigarette into the snow before disappearing with Laura behind an oncoming bus. They climbed on, but I couldn't see either one of them through the bus windows. The winter's mixture of salt and mud had covered the majority of the windows, and the sun's reflection blinded me. What had I done? How would I explain?

I rushed to the nearest tree. I bent over,

threw up my breakfast, and stared at the snow for a moment. I was light-headed and filled with thoughts... too many thoughts.

"Kaity, what's wrong?" I heard Maddi ask.

I felt a gentle hand touch my back, and I tried to focus my eyes, but everything was blurry. I tried to control my breathing.

"Kaity?" Maddi persisted.

I wiped my mouth and slowly stood up.

"Be right back," I said.

And that's when I decided to be a moron. All I could do was run after the bus. I heard the snow slosh underneath my feet as I ran forward, attempting to catch the impossible.

"Kaity, wait!" Maddi shouted.

But I kept running. I heard her run after me, but I didn't care. A burning sensation filled my chest, and I felt my leg muscles weaken. I couldn't stop—I wouldn't. The bus would have to stop again soon, and I would climb on to see her. I was barely two minutes in when I suddenly felt someone jerk me back.

"Stop it!" Maddi shouted. "Where the hell are you going? I can't work alone!"

I bent over, hands on my knees for support, and fought to catch my breath.

"Kaity, what's wrong with you?" Maddi asked.

I turned around and stared at her large, worried blue eyes. Her eyebrows were slanted with sincere concern. She didn't have that usual dimpled-face expression anymore. I fought to keep my composure, but I felt a knot form in my throat. It was coming, and I could feel it. My lower lip quivered and I bowed my head.

"Oh, Kaity," Maddi said and pulled me into her arms.

I cried uncontrollably, holding her tight around the waist. It was extremely embarrassing, but I couldn't help myself. All of these emotions had built up and were stored somewhere deep down. She pressed her hand against my head and tried to calm me.

"It's okay, sweetheart," she said.

When I finally began to regain some self-control, she grabbed my chin and forced my wet eyes to look up at her.

"I think we have something to talk about. How about we go back inside and chat over some pizza?" she said.

I nodded and followed her back to work.

We spent the remainder of the afternoon at the front of the store, me with a box of Kleenex, hiding in the staff room, and Maddi, alternating between the front cash register and my hiding area. I don't know why, but I was completely honest with her about everything. I admitted to being gay. I admitted to being in love. I admitted to not understanding where we'd gone wrong and why Sam had stopped talking to me. It had only been a fight. Why would she cut me out of her life completely? What had I done that was so terrible? I wasn't a bad person, I kept repeating, which only led me to cry some more.

"Sweetheart, look at me," Maddi said, staring at me in a way I'd never seen before. She was so focused, so certain of herself. I looked up and wiped my eyes. "You care about this girl, right?" she asked.

"Right," I blubbered.

"You don't know what went wrong, right?"

"Right," I said.

"Then you have to go ask her. Confront her about it," she said.

"She got rid of her phone," I said and burst into another pathetic crying fit. I didn't know what was wrong with me. I had never cried this much in my life. I was strong. I wasn't a crier.

"Sweetheart, listen," she said and handed me some more Kleenex. "Do you know where she lives?"

"Yeah."

"Then go to her house and talk to her. Or you can keep wondering, and it'll drive you crazy," she said before she squeezed my hand and hugged me.

She was right; she was absolutely right. I needed to know. I couldn't go on living this way, constantly wondering what was on Sam's mind.

"Tonight?" I asked.

Maddi tilted her head, grimaced, and said, "I think she'll need to cool off after today. Let it sit until the weekend. She'll be calmer, and you guys can talk like adults."

"She probably doesn't even care." I almost started crying again when Maddi chuckled.

"Doesn't care? If looks could kill, Kaity, I'd be dead."

I couldn't help but smile at that. Sam had indeed been staring with absolute hatred. Which made me wonder; if I let it sit for a couple of days, wouldn't that worsen things? Wasn't it better to explain everything right now? I bit my lip and contemplated what to do.

"Are you sure I should let it sit?" I asked. "I mean, if she is angry, that's kind of cruel, isn't it?"

"If she drinks the way you say she does, chances are she'll be hammered by the time you get there. You won't be able to talk to her. Trust me."

Maddi was right. I didn't want to speak to drunken Sam; I wanted sober Sam. She would understand and be more willing to listen. I took a deep breath and took a bite of the chocolate bar Maddi had given me as comfort food.

"Thanks, Maddi," I said and smiled up at her, without knowing I had brown chocolate chunks smudged on my upper teeth.

Maddi looked at my smile and laughed.

"Don't worry about it." She looked away, sighed, and added, "Love is really tough, but it's even tougher if you go through it alone."

Chapter 13

The wait for Friday was excruciating. Fortunately, Wednesday was Halloween and I had decided to dress as a fly. Why? Because Maddi had agreed to be a spider.

I found two dark red cardboard plates and drew a bunch of lines across them to mimic fly eyes. I punched two holes for vision and attached the plates onto my face. The only visible feature was now my mouth. It was pretty funny. I then tied my hair into a ponytail and greased it up with hair gel. I wore a shiny turquoise top that I'd found at a local thrift store, along with tight black pants. I wore small, round wings that were initially intended for a fairy costume. Who would know?

When I walked into work, I couldn't help but laugh at Maddi's costume. She wore all black material with four extra arms attached to her shirt and pants. Her face was entirely black, and she had drawn a bunch of white eyes around her own. It was hilarious. When she saw me enter, she made a weird *click click click* sound with her tongue and tried to crawl her way over to me on four legs (well, eight). I burst into ridiculous laughter and ran away from the creepy bug.

"Bzzzz!" I hummed, running around in circles. But before I knew it, I was entangled in a mess of webs.

"Got you! You stupid fly! Now I feast!" she growled and started chewing on my arm.

"Get off!" I yelled. I couldn't catch my breath due to all of the laughter.

Although amusing, it became embarrassing when an old woman walked in and stared at us from behind her thick glasses. We straightened ourselves and Maddi asked if she needed any help. I made my way to my cash register, still attempting to free myself from Maddi's sticky trap. I couldn't quite tell what it was. Silly String? It must have been.

I eventually removed the plates from my face, because it became difficult to see the transactions I was processing. I had handed out the wrong change several times, only to be corrected. I now resembled a homeless grease bag from the eighties—excellent!

"What are you doing tonight?" Maddi asked. Her makeup was beginning to smudge, so it looked as though she had cried white tears.

"Nothing planned. Probably handing out candy at my place," I said, smirking at her makeup.

"Stop it." She laughed. "Well, you should come over. My roommate and I are throwing a little get-together. Beer, candy, and scary movies."

"Oh, um," I said.

I'm not certain why I hesitated. Perhaps it was because I hadn't socialized in what felt like forever. I was somewhat nervous to attend a party where I knew no one. Although this was true, I believe the deeper reason for my uncertainty lay in the fact that there was going to be alcohol. Would the partying remind me more of Sam? Or would I get so drunk that I would show up at Sam's place? *Relax*, I told myself. I wasn't an alcoholic. I simply wouldn't get drunk. So I graciously accepted her offer.

"Great! So this is where I live," she said, writing down a bunch of information on a piece of paper, including her cell phone number and the start time—seven p.m.

"If you come early enough, we can hand out candy to the little kids. Don't forget to keep your costume."

I looked down at the little slip she gave me and smiled.

"That sounds awesome, thanks."

I was actually excited. I hadn't mingled with people in a very long time, and I was now undeniably overdue for some socializing.

When I arrived home, I rushed upstairs and cleaned my hair. I removed my ugly clothes and instead, put on a pair of jeans and a nice white T-shirt. With my eyeliner, I did what I had seen done on an episode of *The Office* and wrote the word BOOK across my face. This was the most effortless costume I could think of—Facebook. And it was sure to get a few laughs.

I hopped on the bus around and made my way to the address Maddi had provided. The sun had already set and kids were roaming the streets with their parents. There were pumpkins and dry leaves on every lawn. The trees were still coated with snow, but the weather was surprisingly mild. I finally found Maddi's house and knocked on the front door.

"Hey there," said some Hulk-dressed guy as he opened the door, "where's your candy bag?"

I opened my mouth to explain myself, but his jaw dropped open to release a very loud, overly-exaggerated laugh.

"Come on in, come on in!" he said, wrapping an arm around my neck. "Kaitlyn, right? Or Kaity, if you prefer. I'm Joshua. The Hulk, tonight. What are you?" he asked, stopping in his steps.

I faced him and smiled.

"I don't get it," he said.

"Facebook," I said and he burst into that same, wide-mouthed laughter.

"I like you already, Kaitlyn," he said.

What a personality, I thought. Was he drunk? I noticed the can of Brisk in his hand. He wasn't even drinking.

"Kaity!" I heard Maddi call out. "You made it!"

She hugged me and led me into the kitchen.

"What do you want? We have Cosmos, Smirnoff, Blue... you name it."

I nearly asked for a Blue but thought it best to stay away from beer. There were too many memories linked to it. So I asked for a Smirnoff, instead.

She gave me a tour of the place and guided me to the basement, where everyone was gathered. They were all in their twenties, which was somewhat intimidating for me. I wasn't used to being around such a young crowd. I was introduced to the majority of the people and knew I'd eventually meet the rest throughout the night. I planned to return home around eleven so that I'd get adequate sleep for work the next day.

Everyone I spoke with turned out to be extremely friendly. Most were open, social people—not at all the same atmosphere I'd found at Sam's parties. The goal here wasn't to get drunk. Of course, most people had a drink in their hands, but everyone appeared to be sober. I had only been taught to get drunk; therefore, I didn't quite understand the concept of social drinking. But I would have to try.

I traveled to the kitchen a few times to refresh my beverage, only to tumble into more conversations. I much preferred staying on the main floor, since Maddi's kitchen was extremely clean. The basement, I found, was too clustered with people. I had everything up here; fresh air, conversation, a chair, and an unlimited supply of alcohol.

By the time eleven o'clock came around, my plan had been destroyed. I was already seeing double, and I could hear myself slurring. How did I manage to get so drunk? This wasn't good; I had to work the next day. But right now, I didn't care. I didn't want to think; I wanted to remain numb. I had missed this sensation so much—this unwillingness to participate in feeling the depth of my emotions. I was free again. And to remain so, I drank some more.

I suddenly heard a knock at my door and forced my eyes open. Where the hell was I? Where had the party gone?

"Kaitlyn?" I heard someone say.

I looked around, utterly bewildered. *What? Where?* I suddenly saw Amy standing at my door. I was home. I was in my room.

"Are you okay? Work called. Why didn't you go?" she asked.

"What?" My eyes widened at the sight of my bedside clock. Shit! It was past noon.

"What happened to you?" Amy asked.

I dropped back into bed and pressed my fingers against my throbbing temples. What had I done? I had missed work. I felt so ashamed.

"Do you want me to call work for you?" she asked.

"No, no," I said quickly, "I'll take care of it. Thanks."

Amy left and closed the door. I searched around and finally found my phone. I had a bunch of missed calls, both from Maddi's cell phone and from Lacey's Pharmacy. What would I tell her? That I had blacked out? That I was hungover? What had I done last night? I was uncertain whether the nausea I felt was alcohol-induced or stress-related, but I suddenly thought about Sam. Had I tried to go to her house? I was going to be sick. I curled up in a ball and went back to sleep.

When I woke up again, I had an extra five missed calls from Maddi. This was it. I had to call her back. So I dialed her number and wiped the cotton from the corner of my lips.

"Kaity? Kaity! What the hell happened to you?" Maddi asked.

"Hey, Maddi, I'm so sorry I didn't come in." I felt terrible. Was David going to fire me because of this?

"Sweetheart, don't worry about it. You were upset," she said.

"I was?"

"You don't remember?" she asked.

Ugh. I felt sick again. This inability to recollect last night's events killed me. My silence had given her enough of an answer.

"You were crying all night."

"I was drunk. I'm sorry," I said. I felt so foolish—so humiliated.

"Don't be sorry. It's okay. You wanted to see Sam."

"Did I?" I asked.

"No. I didn't let you. Joshua drove you home," she said. "Did you call her?"

"Her phone doesn't work anymore. I couldn't have," I said.

That was a relief. I asked her to thank Joshua for me. I must have sounded so pathetic, so defeated. I'd made a complete ass of myself and I was humiliated.

"Look, don't sweat it, okay? I've gotten way too drunk many times before. It happens to everyone," she said and laughed it off. "As long as you're all right."

"I'm good. Hungover, but good," I admitted.

She laughed, and I promised to make it to

work the next day. I hung up and went back to sleep, still thoroughly disgusted with myself. When I awoke for supper, I was surprised that no one bothered to ask me what I had done for Halloween. It was as if I didn't exist. What were they assuming? That I'd gone off and had sex with a girl? Come on. It was ridiculous how distant my family had become, as if they were repulsed by my very existence. Out of sight, out of mind was their motto.

The only thing that kept me sane was the fact that the next day would be Friday, which meant I would go see Sam. I had to. I couldn't sit around anymore, wondering, hoping.

Maddi was very sweet with me when I came in Friday morning. She didn't bring up the party or my absence the previous day.

"Hey, look at this," she said, showing me a bottle of body lotion.

"What is it?" I asked.

"It's the new firming lotion we received. Firms up your legs. I think I'm gonna buy some and try it out."

I shook my head and laughed. "I don't know if that stuff really works."

"Well, we're just gonna have to find out, aren't we?" she said.

Although my day was quite ordinary, I had a very disturbing knot in my abdomen. Sam. She was all I could think about. How would she react when I knocked on her door? Would she tell me to go home? Would she even be there? Would she ignore me, altogether? I remembered her standing out in the cold across the street, her eyes so intense. The mere image in my mind weakened my legs. She had the most unbelievable ability to make me feel like Jello—nothing but soft, boneless Jello.

"You should go see her right now, before Friday night kicks in," Maddi said.

"Right now?" I nearly choked. "I'll never be back on time."

"Not over your lunch, silly. Just go. I'll cover for you. You don't have to come back."

I looked at the clock; it was 1:30. *Before Friday night kicks in?* I was certain that Maddi was referring to Sam's party lifestyle. If I showed up at her door late Friday night, chances were she wouldn't even be home. Either that, or she would be too drunk to talk to me. I didn't want to risk that. I had to see her. I needed to hear her speak.

"Go on!" She shooed me away. "Suck it up, take a deep breath, and dive right in. You'll feel better after. I promise."

I gulped and stared at her.

"Kaity, what's the worst that could happen? She'll tell you to fuck off? Who cares? That's basically how you're feeling right now, anyways. It may as well have already happened."

Maddi was right. It couldn't get any worse than this. So I thanked her profusely, grabbed my jacket, and rushed out into the piercing autumn wind.

I wanted to vomit during the entire bus ride to Sam's place. She was still living there, wasn't she? There would have been no reason for her to move. Oh no. What if Laura was there? What if Laura beat me up? She was extremely defensive. I tried my best to erase all of these negative thoughts. There was no use overthinking anything. Whatever happened, happened. That was it. I transferred buses and found myself five minutes away from her place. This was tough. My heart raced. I could feel the adrenaline rushing throughout my body, causing my hands to tremble. *Just do it*, I told myself.

And before I knew it, I was walking towards Sam's house. Its old, brown-and-white exterior was still the same as it had been when I first saw it. I couldn't tell whether or not anyone was home, but I was about to find out. I walked up the stairs and stared at the door for a moment. I considered turning around and running the other way, but I was in too deep now. I folded my trembling fingers into a fist and knocked on the door. The wait was excruciating. I clenched my jaw and tried my best to remain still, but I could feel my entire body shaking. Whether this was brought on by the cold or by my nerves, I couldn't quite tell.

I heard the lock turn, and I nearly fainted. Someone was there. The door slowly opened and a pair of blue eyes looked up at me.

"Oh, hey," Travis said.

His hair was all over the place, and his eyes were so tired, so heavy looking. He looked as though he had gotten run over by a bus the night before. A hangover, I assumed.

"Hey," I said, "is Sam here?"

"Yeah man, she's in her room," he said and opened the door, before disappearing into the kitchen.

The house was a mess. There were beer bottles everywhere, dirty ashtrays, and filthy laundry lying around. I nearly jumped against the wall when I noticed Laura passed out on the sofa, one arm and one leg dangling to the floor.

I slowly walked towards Sam's room, my heart aching. So many thoughts rushed through my mind. Would I find her lying with another girl? Had she turned around, out of spite, and found someone herself, thinking that I was already involved with another person? What would I say? Would she be happy to see me? My thoughts ended there, because I reached for the door handle and quietly stepped inside.

To my unfortunate surprise, two people

were lying in the bed. I froze. Sam's long black hair was everywhere, and she was facing the wall. Beside her was another person—guy or girl, I couldn't tell—whose face was pressed into the pillow. I took a step back, preparing to exit the room, when the other person's head jolted up and her eyes met mine.

"Oh. Hey dude," she said.

It was Jo. Laura's friend: the girl I'd met downtown before entering Taylor's Tower. Had they had...? Had she left me for her? Why was Jo here? I couldn't speak. I stared at her, my mouth half-open. She moaned loudly and sat upright, her spiked hair flattened on one side. Her clothes were all on, which was a good sign.

Her shifting caused Sam to grunt and wiggle around a bit, until I finally heard Sam speak.

"Jo, what the fuck? Get out of my bed," she moaned, still facing the wall.

"Dude, I don't sleep on floors. Give me a break," Jo said, trying to fix her hair. "Was she always this bitchy with you, Kaity?" she asked, elevating her tired eyes my way.

I swallowed hard. Sam swung backward so quickly that her hair followed her swift movement, and her gaze landed on me. Her eyes were so bright, so vibrant. I couldn't speak.

"Jo, get out," Sam said.

"Yo man, chill. I need my smokes."

"I SAID GET OUT!" Sam shouted and pushed

Jo off of the bed.

Jo stumbled on all fours, then finally stood up, but nearly fell against me before she exited the room. I couldn't move. I just stood there, staring at Sam.

"Close my door," Sam said.

So I walked in and did as I was told. Without another thought, I calmly walked her way and sat on the bed.

"I... I... That girl, I'm not with... She's my friend, Maddi. We were joking around... I, Sam, I swear. She's not even gay. I..." I tried, but I knew that I wouldn't get very far.

Tears came pouring out of my eyes. Sam's arms swung around my neck and she pulled me against her body. I cried into her neck, and she held me tight—tighter than she had ever held me before. We didn't speak. We simply lay there, conscious of each other's breathing—appreciative of each other's presence.

Chapter 14

"Hey," I heard Sam say.

I opened my eyes. She was awake, just watching me.

"Hey," I said back.

"I'm sorry."

"Me too," I said and looked down.

"No, it's my fault. You didn't do anything wrong."

I didn't answer.

"When I was mad at you that day, you drank by yourself, which made me realize, that, well," she paused, "it meant you actually cared about me. It scared me. I'm so sorry Kaity."

"Why would it scare you? Isn't care a good thing?" I asked.

"It is, I guess. But not when everyone you've ever cared about has left you," she said.

I knew that the term *everyone* included her aunt, but surely, there was much more to Sam that I didn't know about.

"My dad's fat," she said.

I smiled up at her, on the verge of laughter. Where was she going with this?

"Well, he used to be. He lives alone somewhere in Montreal. I'm not even sure where. Last I heard, he barely has any teeth left, and he's addicted to crystal meth."

Okay. So this hadn't been a joke. My smile turned into a frown, but I remained silent.

"My mom's thin."

I blinked.

"Well, the last time I saw her, anyway. I have no idea where she is. She left when I was seven. I saw her again at fourteen when I was visiting a friend in Ottawa. She was drunk and prostituting downtown."

I was speechless. What was I supposed to say? I wanted to console her, but I didn't feel that now was the time. I looked away and bit my tongue.

"My brother's pale," she said.

At this, I looked up again. Was he sick? In the hospital?

"He rarely sees sunlight. He's in jail. He's twenty-four. Got busted for trafficking cocaine into the States."

She looked away from me and closed her eyes. I detected something glossy sliding down her cheek. A tear. Sam's tear. I had never seen her cry before. She was tough—so brave and aggressive by nature. She wasn't the type to shed a tear for anyone or anything. I placed an open palm against her face and kissed her forehead.

"I'm so sorry, Sam," I said and meant it more than anything.

This girl was so damaged. All of my family issues suddenly seemed so minuscule in comparison to hers. I had a marvelous life—I had absolutely nothing to complain about. My parents were still together, I had a great home, a full-time job, and a healthy body. A pang of unavoidable guilt crept into my conscience.

"It's okay," she said.

I squeezed her hard.

"I want to try," she said.

"Try what?"

"To be your girlfriend."

Did she mean it? Was she going to leave me again in a week? How could I be certain? But it didn't matter, because she would try. And that was all I could really ask for.

"I'd like that," I said. I wanted to scream. To sing.

"Kaity?"

"Yeah?"

"I know this is kind of sudden, and I hate to be a U-Hauler, but I want to move out with you."

This was definitely sudden. I tried to remain quiet for a moment as if I were contemplating the idea, even though all I wanted to do was shout *yes*. But then another thought crossed my mind—why move out and pay rent when this place was already paid for? It was idiotic, really.

"But this house is paid for."

"Exactly. I'm gonna sell it. It'll give me plenty enough to take care of you. Besides, if I continue the way I'm doing, I'm going to end up dying the same way my aunt did. I don't want to live in this memory anymore."

Was this real? It had to be. No way was she drunk and talking nonsense. She was sober; I could see it in her eyes. And every word was sincere.

"You know I want to live with you," I said, wanting to jump out of my own body.

Want to? I wanted nothing more than this! I couldn't believe it! How had we gone from not talking to suddenly planning a future together? This didn't make the slightest bit of sense to me.

She smiled at me, her perfect face lighting up. "I'll get a new phone, too."

I snorted. "That explains a bit. What happened to yours?"

"I got angry, so I threw it in the lake down the street."

162

"Thank you," I said, looking up at her from behind slanted eyebrows.

"What for?"

"For not hating me," I said.

"Please," she snorted, "I couldn't hate you if I tried."

Chapter 15

"Hey Kaity, look. I'm out," Sam said, stepping out of the huge, mirrored-door closet.

I burst into laughter and threw my arms around her neck.

"Ew, get off me you big ol' dyke!" she said. She shoved me away and wrinkled her nose.

"Shut up," I laughed, "you're one to talk, you're as straight as a rainbow."

She pulled me back into her arms, but we were interrupted by the little woman with curly red hair, whose name I had completely forgotten.

"So, what do you girls think?" the woman asked, her eyes scoping the empty apartment.

"I think it's gorgeous. What do you think?" Sam asked, glancing back at me.

"Agreed," I said.

"So the rent is nine hundred and eighty dollars per month, excluding hydro. It's a wonderful neighborhood, and there are plenty of nice young fellows who go out to play soccer every weekend at the park," she said, winking at us.

I nearly threw up.

"That's great," Sam said, utterly disinterested, "maybe they can point us to the nearest sex shop so I can buy a strap-on for me and my girlfriend."

She threw her arm over my shoulder and hugged me close. My eyes bulged and I felt my face go red. The woman cleared her throat and clenched her fingers around her clipboard.

"Well, um. Maybe they can. I'm going to need to do a record check, and then the place is yours if you want it."

Sam tilted her head and grinned pretentiously. The woman showed us out, tight-lipped until we reached the front doors of the apartment building.

"Well, I'll keep in touch," the woman said and walked away.

The moment we were of reasonable distance away from the landlord, I slapped Sam on the shoulder and glared at her.

"Aw, you're so cute," she said.

"Why'd you do that?" I asked.

"That place was a shit hole, and I wanted to have a bit of fun."

"I thought it was nice," I said.

"Well clearly, you don't think too well," she said, a mischievous smirk on her face.

We walked a little further down the street—two blocks down—and arrived at an exquisite high-rise apartment building.

"This is it," Sam said, looking down at her printed notes.

I couldn't believe my eyes. The place was statuesque. Everything was so clean and shiny. According to Sam, the rent was about one thousand dollars a month.

The room was just as remarkable as the building. It was a one-bedroom, which was all we needed, and it was quite spacious. We were within walking distance to downtown and had an exquisite view from the balcony.

"Looks like we found our place," Sam said and kissed me on the lips.

Needless to say, we got the apartment. It was now only a matter of filling out forms and reference checks.

Our next mission was to shop for household goods—dishes, utensils, tables, sofas, a microwave, and Tupperware. Fortunately, Sam wasn't going to bother bringing anything from her aunt's place, so there was no need for heavy lifting. Sam gave Mel and Travis a two-week notice to find another place to stash their drugs. It was short notice, but they would survive.

* * *

"Well, well, well. You look happy. How was the chat?" Maddi asked as I entered work Monday morning.

I couldn't hide my grin, as much as I tried.

"It went well," I said.

"Well? Please. Look at you. You look like a gay boy who just won a thousand dollars' worth of hair products."

I laughed.

"Are you saying I look like a boy?" I asked.

"Shut up. Tell me everything. What happened?" she asked, rushing over to me.

"I don't know. I mean, we talked, and, well, things just kind of fell into place really fast. She said she missed me, and..."

"Awww!" Maddi shouted.

I smirked. "Shut up."

"That's too cute," she said.

"So, we're moving in together," I said.

Her brows came close together. "Seriously? You don't think that's a little soon? How long have you known this girl?"

"A few months. I know. I know it's too soon, but it feels right. I can't explain it. Besides, I need to move out, and so does she."

Maddi stared at me, opened her mouth, but then bit down on her bottom lip.

"What?" I asked.

"Please be careful, I mean..." she said.

"I know, I know. I will be; I promise." I didn't want to hear a speech. All I wanted in return from Maddi was to hear that she was happy for me.

"Kaity, once you move in with someone, it's hard to get out of it," she said.

I was getting frustrated. Why wasn't she supporting me? I didn't want to hear the what-ifs. I wanted her to be as excited as I was.

"I won't want to get out of it," I said, my tone hardening.

"Look, I'm only telling you to be careful, that's all. I'm happy for you, I am. All I'm asking is that you be careful."

"And I will be!" I said. I hadn't meant to sound so defensive.

"Kaity, don't get mad at me," she said. She took a deep breath and exhaled. "I'm only telling you this because I moved in with a stoner years ago. In the end, he picked the drug over me, and it was a really big mess. It hurt more than you can imagine. I just don't want you to go through anything like that."

I blinked. Poor Maddi. I could tell it still hurt. She must have deeply cared about this boy.

"I'm sorry, really," I said. "But... Sam's different. I just know it."

She forced a smile and squeezed my shoulder. "You're probably right."

We didn't speak much for the remainder of the day. Had I upset her by picking at an old scab? I understood that she was worried about me, but her past disasters had nothing to do with my present life. Everyone's different, people are all different. It's impossible to compare situations. Sam wasn't that bad. Did she drink a lot? Yes. But only because she had nothing better to do with her time. Things would change, I knew they would. I wished Maddi could see what I saw in Sam.

After all the paperwork was finally completed, we were granted the keys to our new apartment. There wasn't much to bring, and I managed to pack the majority of my belongings in one suitcase.

It was a sunny Wednesday afternoon, and I had just finished work. Having only lived in our new place for a few days, I was itching all day to go home—our home. But when I walked through our apartment door, I didn't receive the welcome I'd anticipated. The moment I walked in, I spotted Sam sitting on the floor, playing cards by herself with a beer in one hand. What was she doing? Suddenly, I wanted to tear the beer away from her and smash the bottle into hundreds of pieces. Sure, we drank on weekends together, but on a Wednesday afternoon? What was the reason? It was midweek. Why did I suddenly feel this anger towards her drinking? She wasn't Maddi's ex-boyfriend. She wasn't a drunk. She was only bored and was enjoying one drink. I took a deep breath and cracked one open myself.

"Hey," I said. I fought with myself.

Don't be angry. Don't be angry. Look at that face. She's perfect.

"Hey honey," she said, getting up. She kissed my cheek.

I offered her a playful smirk. "What are you doing?"

"Playing solitaire. We have a bunch of stuff coming in a few hours. I bought a sofa, a loveseat, a huge flat-screen TV, a DVD player, a PS3, and a bunch more!"

I hugged her tight. This was definitely good news. I looked around at the empty apartment. It felt so lonely. I couldn't imagine how anyone lived alone. I was so thrilled to have Sam here with me.

"Hey, you want to throw a housewarming party Friday night?" she asked.

I thought about it for a moment and glanced down at the beer in her hand, but shook my irrational thoughts away and smiled up at her.

"Let's go shopping for decorations and all of that this week," she said. She was so excited, it made me happy.

By Friday evening, our apartment was filled with paintings; plants; new kitchen essentials; a leather sofa and loveseat; a few tables; a huge fifty-inch TV; a DVD player; a PS3; an enormous, high-quality sound system in which an iPod could be inserted; an extremely comfortable king-size bed; and a minifridge filled with drinks for our party. We set up a few bowls of chips and cheese puffs on the table, along with a forty of vodka surrounded by a dozen shot glasses.

In other words, we were prepared.

Maddi was due to arrive soon with a few of her friends. I had invited her Thursday, and Sam had taken the liberty of inviting as many people as possible. I dressed in something a little more presentable and poured myself a rum and Coke. The smooth, burning sensation helped calm my nerves. I hadn't bothered to call Matt or anyone else from school. I would stick with my plan—my old life was over (well, apart from Sam). I suddenly felt Sam's cold hand grab my wrist. She swung me around. I looked at her, surprised.

"Stop it," she said, smirking at me.

"Stop what?" I smiled.

"Stop being so nervous; it's a party."

"That obvious, huh?" I asked, and took another chug of my drink.

"Relax," she said soothingly.

She leaned in and massaged my shoulders, her hot breath beating against the back of my neck. She slid her hand down my stomach, along my hips, and then along my thigh. My knees weakened and I closed my eyes. I appreciated every touch, every breath. But before anything else could happen, she abruptly removed her hands and pushed me away.

"We don't have time for that," she said.

I smiled dreamily and shook my head. I felt so dizzy, so drugged. What a tease. I blinked a few times to regain my senses, took another sip of my drink, and said, "You're an ass."

"I know, but you like it," she said, stuck her tongue out at me, and disappeared into the kitchen to pour herself a drink. She was right; I did like it.

The apartment was buzzing by around nine o'clock. I couldn't believe how many people she had invited. How did she know so many people? I noticed Laura enter. She hugged Sam around the neck and kissed her cheek. My jaw clenched. I knew they had no romantic history, but I couldn't fight this feeling. I felt as though Laura cared about Sam more than she led on.

"Hey girl," Laura said to me.

"Oh, hey," I stammered.

Although it had been a while since Laura's jealous outburst, all I could remember was the way she had freaked out when Sam refused to help her score more drugs through prostitution. I was still somewhat angry, knowing that Laura had influenced Sam into doing something so horrible. I didn't much appreciate the fact that Sam was still friends with her. She was jealous and psychotic. She smiled at me before walking away, and I knew very well how pretentious she was being. She didn't like me at all. Why? It was either because I was her drug-block, or whatever it is you'd call that, or, it was because she wanted Sam.

Jo was also there. She sported a sleek, black suit with a red tie. I greeted her, along with every other random guest who entered the apartment. I was so relieved when Maddi walked through the door. Finally! Someone I knew!

"Hey!" I exclaimed and ran her way.

She offered the goofiest smile and pulled me in for a hug. She introduced me to her couple friends: Rebecca, Louise, Adam, and Pete. It was easy to determine who was together—Rebecca was holding onto Pete as if her life depended on it. And I didn't blame her, because Pete was very handsome.

"Nice to meet you guys," I said.

"Here!" Maddi shouted.

Her tone took me aback and I blinked at her when she shoved an oddly shaped package in front of my face.

"What is it?" I asked.

"A housewarming gift. Duh," she said.

I shook my head and opened the bag. It was an adorable, little bonsai tree. "That's too cute! Thanks, Maddi" I hugged her again.

"No problem." She winked and tapped me on the cheek. "Hey, maybe tonight it'll be my turn to get shit-faced and do something dumb," she added.

"Har har har," I said, staring at her dully.

"Oh, I'm only teasing. Don't be such a tart," she said.

I showed her around, although it was difficult to make it through the crowd which had so quickly assembled. The music blared and it seemed as though everyone was trying to talk over the noise—which, quite obviously, they were. I ran into the strangest people as I walked around my apartment.

"I'm Danny. Cool party," one man said.

He must have been in his mid-twenties. He had a piercing across the bridge of his nose, his ears were entirely masked in silver, and his gray eyes were outlined with blue eyeliner. Although I do not consider myself judgmental, I knew I assumed the worst in him. I was extremely surprised when he told me he had been clean for well over five years and that he was now offering his time to volunteer organizations. He sipped his iced tea and saluted me goodbye right before Sam jumped in out of nowhere and grabbed me around the waist.

"How do you know all of these people?" I asked.

Her warm breath slid along the curve of my ear.

"Ah, you know. Here and there. I can't keep track. And I don't know all of them."

I wasn't sure what to think. She had told me her old life was behind her. But was it really? I wondered if most of these people had contributed to the trouble Sam got into as a teenager. I looked around. Tattoos, piercings, angry stares. Was I being judgmental again? Probably.

I glanced behind me when I heard Maddi laugh. She was sitting on the sofa, surrounded by three larger men who were *cheersing* her drink. I was glad she wasn't uncomfortable here. After all, this wasn't your typical high school crowd. I suddenly remembered the first party Sam had invited me to at her place. It had been the same story. No one seemed to care about the crowd's age variation.

"All right, time for the gifts!" a woman shouted. One of Sam's old friends, I assumed.

Gifts? I glanced her way and noticed a pile of horribly wrapped presents lying in the corner of the apartment. How had I not noticed these? Everyone gathered, and Sam made her presence known.

"Okay guys, si'down!" she shouted.

I sat on the loveseat, my sight now doubled. It seemed as though only minutes ago I had been sober. I looked around and found Maddi sitting on the other side, smiling at me. I returned the joy, but I wondered if she had genuinely meant it. Did she still believe that my moving in with Sam was a mistake? Had it been a mistake?

I rolled my eyes towards Sam again and watched as she shook the presents around with a huge, goofy grin on her face. I was unable to doubt my decision at this point—she was so beautiful. How could this have possibly been a mistake? *Look at her!* I wanted to tell Maddi. *Just look at her!* Why couldn't she see what I saw?

Sam's round eyes fell onto me for a second, and I felt my stomach turn. Not long ago, this girl had been so cold to me in class. I couldn't believe how rapidly things had changed.

"Kaity!" Sam shouted.

I was shaken out of my daze when she shoved a microwave in my face.

Before I could speak, she interrupted. "I know we already have one, but this one is going in our room. You know, for those mornings when we don't want to get out of bed."

I laughed and grabbed the big box. As I read the details, I spotted Maddi's bright eyes staring at me in an unusual way. They were so sad, as if aware of something I wasn't. Why was she doing this? I was trying to have a good time. I didn't care about her past wounds right now. This wasn't the time. I almost spoke my thoughts aloud, due to my lack of inhibition, but a resonant knock at the door interrupted me.

Chapter 16

"Look, I'm not going to ask you twice. If you guys can't keep it down, we're going to evacuate the apartment ourselves," said the police officer.

He was an extremely buff-looking cop, with his arms crossed over his chest and his square chin elevated higher than his neck. Beside him stood his partner, a very butch-looking cop. Although she was smaller, I knew it would be wisest not to anger her. She looked like the aggressive type.

"Fuck man, we're trying to have a housewarming party," Sam said. She shot a glance into the kitchen and said, "It's eleven o'clock on a Friday night. Who the hell is complaining about noise?"

"After this room is evacuated, I'll have no problem taking you with us to the station," said the officer.

I saw Sam roll her eyes, and all I wanted to do was shake her. What the hell was she doing? Why was it that no matter where we were, she had some way of attracting trouble?

"Dude, come back after the party." Sam tried to slam the door closed, but the cop's steel-toe boot got in the way.

"I don't think so," he said and forced his way into the apartment.

"Wait!" Maddi said. "Can I talk to you guys outside?"

She stared desperately at the police, waiting for a yes.

"You'd better not be wasting our time," said the female cop. The menace in her voice had accurately matched her appearance.

"No, I'm not. I promise," Maddi assured them.

"Maddi, give it a rest. These pig…" Sam tried, but I grabbed her by the shirt and forced her into the kitchen.

I had never been physical with her, and I was afraid of how she was going to react, but I knew that it had to be done. I didn't want her going to prison.

"What the fuck?" she snapped. She rolled her eyes up at me. They were so red—so tired. She was inarguably drunk.

"Sam, let Maddi take care of it, okay? Please," I said, trying to sound as sweet as possible. The last thing I wanted was a fight.

"What? So you think Maddi is better than me? Is that it?" she asked.

She shoved me back with both hands, and I hit my head against the wooden handle of the kitchen cupboard. I squinted and felt my throat tighten. I wasn't too hurt, at least not physically. I couldn't believe that she had just intentionally harmed me. This wasn't Sam. I stared at the floor with my hand pressed against my head. Luckily, no one had seen what happened.

"Kaity," Sam said. Her narrowed eyes widened, and I knew that guilt was kicking in. She grabbed my head and hugged me close. "I'm so sorry."

I didn't talk. I stood stiff, uncertain of my feelings. I wasn't angry, I was hurt—afraid, even. She had been so irrational. How had she gone about creating a nonexistent problem with the use of her imagination? I wiped my wet cheeks and surrendered to her soft hands, because there was no one else to console me.

"Kaity?" Maddi asked.

She stood by the kitchen entrance, staring at me. I sniffled the remainder of my emotions and tried my best to smile at her.

"So, what happened?" I asked.

She ignored my question and asked, "You guys okay?"

"We're fine," Sam said and walked away.

I stood there alone, my hands lingering in front of me in an awkward position now that Sam had left.

"What happened?" Maddi whispered.

She approached me with such tenderness. Her worried eyes scanned my face, and she grabbed my hand.

"Nothing. Just a little fight. Seriously, it's okay," I said and forced a pathetic smile.

"You sure?"

"Yeah. What happened out there? Where are the cops?" I asked, purposely avoiding the subject at hand.

"I told them I'd take care of it," she said, squeezed my shoulder, and made her way into the living room. The volume of the music decreased, and Maddi spoke up. "Everyone, listen up!"

To my surprise, everyone did as told and stopped talking.

"If we don't keep it down, we're getting kicked out. So let's try to keep a reasonable volume, okay?" Maddi said.

There were a few whispers and mutters among the crowd, but as a whole, they obeyed. Sam finished the gifts as if nothing had happened between us. She grinned at me whenever something really useful was unwrapped and continued on with her humorous comments. I have to admit that the party had become lame due to our volume restriction, but I was still thankful to have so many people there supporting us. By midnight, our guests were already leaving to go downtown, where the "real fun" was at.

I'd love to describe the remainder of my night, but to be honest, I don't remember anything specific. I remember hugging Maddi goodbye and her whispering something very important in my ear. I remember getting dressed into something a little classier for the club. I remember catching a cab. And I remember bright lights and loud bass music.

I woke up the next morning, my eyes sealed shut. I moaned at the realization that I was undergoing yet another hangover. So, I rolled over to see Sam, but she wasn't there. Had I lost her last night? Had she gone somewhere else? And at that moment, it was as though all of my hangover symptoms were placed on hold; I jumped out of bed and ran into the living room.

"Sam?" I called out.

She was nowhere to be seen. I searched the bathroom—empty. I ran back into the room and checked the floor by her side of the bed (she could have fallen over, you never know) but she wasn't there, either. So I ran into the kitchen, prepared to search every cabinet when I realized how silly I was being. I paced around, contemplating every possibility. She still didn't have a cell phone, so I had no way of contacting her. I rushed back into the bedroom and opened my phone. No missed calls, nothing. Shit, shit, shit!

I dragged myself back into the living room and dropped onto the soft sofa cushions. What was I going to do? She'd be back soon, wouldn't she? I sighed heavily and rubbed my moistened palms against my forehead. A muffled groan suddenly echoed beside me.

I glanced at the sofa, where a pair of dark-socked feet stuck out. What the hell? I jumped up, cautiously approaching the feet.

"Sam?"

Another groan.

I stretched my neck and spotted dark, messy hair. It was Sam! She was curled up in a fetal position, surrounded by empty beer bottles. At least she was producing sound. Had she not been moving, I would have assumed the worst.

"Sam," I repeated.

"What?" she moaned.

"What the hell are you doing there?"

"Mm..." she said.

It was hopeless. I went into the kitchen and poured her a large glass of water. She accepted it but didn't drink. She lay there, pathetic and vulnerable. I wanted to slap her for having gotten so drunk, but I couldn't. That would have been hypocritical. Instead, I crawled to the floor, pressed my body against hers, and went back to sleep.

I woke up feeling a bit better aside from a stiff neck, and Sam was still asleep beside me. I remember thinking, *I'm never going to drink again*, but somehow, I found myself singing into the neck of a beer bottle by six o'clock, with Sam as my drummer against the kitchen counter. We conjured up the most ridiculous tunes and then ordered another two-four when we realized there were only five beers left.

By ten o'clock I was stumbling into the bathroom to pee. When I was done, Sam was waiting for me, a familiar, drunken smile on her face. She was so perfect. I leaned forward and pressed my lips against hers. She caressed my neck, my arms, then grabbed my hand and led me into the bedroom.

Chapter 17

"How's the new place?" Maddi asked.

"It's great," I said and placed my bag behind the counter.

I felt weird around Maddi now. It seemed as though she were trying to destroy my relationship with Sam. Was this irrational? Most likely. She was just being a friend, but I couldn't alter the way I felt.

There wasn't much conversation that day, and all I could focus on was my desire to return to Sam. I wondered what she was doing. She didn't work at the moment, but she had promised to search for a job, regardless of how much money she now had in the bank.

I finished my shift, said goodbye to Maddi, hopped on the bus, and returned home to my girlfriend. I was excited as I made my way up the apartment stairs. I would jump into her arms and hold her tight. But the desire left me the moment I opened the door. Sam was sitting in the living room with Laura, a deck of playing cards in front of them on the coffee table, along with a huge bottle of gold rum. Cigarette smoke clouded the apartment, and there were dirty dishes everywhere. I took a deep breath and walked forward.

"Hey honey," Sam said and smiled up at me.

I didn't smile back. Why was I so angry? Did I even have reason to be angry? She inhaled another puff of smoke and knocked on the table.

"Damn it!" Laura shouted and threw her cards across the table.

Sam laughed and put her cigarette out in what appeared to be one of my plastic drinking cups, which my mother had offered to give to me when I moved out. It was only when she looked up at me again, that I realized I was still standing there, glaring at them.

"Bad day?" she asked.

I hadn't wanted to start a fight. I hadn't wanted to be angry. But I couldn't suppress my emotions.

"It's Monday, and here you are, getting drunk with someone who hates me, while I'm at work earning a salary?"

Her eyes narrowed as if she had witnessed some alien phenomenon. She opened her mouth but didn't speak.

"And I thought we agreed to no smoking in the apartment? So, what? When I'm gone, the rules go out the window? Is that it? Couldn't you have done something a little more productive with your day?" I snapped. I looked into the kitchen, where pans and greasy plates had piled up. "Like clean the kitchen, maybe?"

"Kaity, sweetheart, relax," Sam said. She jumped to her feet and reached out to touch my shoulder, but I swung my arm and pushed her away.

"Don't," I said.

"I don't see what the big fucking deal is!" she said.

Somehow, my anger seemed to suddenly evaporate. I couldn't fight her when she was angry. I stood there and listened, wondering if I had, just maybe, overreacted.

"I'm not working; I'm enjoying my time off, okay?" she said, now glaring at me.

I wanted to point out that she had never had a real job, but I knew that this wasn't the time to discuss it.

"Couldn't you have invited someone else?" I asked, throwing a stiff finger in Laura's direction. I realized that this had been a mistake, but there was no turning back now.

"Laura's my friend," Sam said coldly.

"Please. She's nothing but an addict happily accepting a free buzz," I said and walked into the bedroom, slamming the door shut.

I fell onto our bed, my face reddening. I was afraid that Sam would come after me, but at the same time, I was proud of having spoken my mind. Laura hated me. She probably insulted me behind my back, yet Sam still had the balls to bring her into our home. It was a slap in the face. Laura would break us up the moment an opportunity came forth. I could see it in her eyes every time she looked at me.

I rationalized my feelings by placing myself in Sam's position. Had Maddi ever called Sam a bitch or yelled at me for being with her, I would have stopped talking to Maddi a long time ago. But Sam didn't seem to care about my feelings.

I heard a few whispers and the apartment door close. There was a light tap at the bedroom door, and Sam slowly entered the room.

"You okay, tiger?" she asked, a little smirk on her face.

Although still upset, I couldn't keep a straight face. I smiled up at her and shrugged.

"Listen, I'm sorry. You're right. No smoking in the apartment, and I know you and Laura don't like each other. She is still my friend though," Sam said.

"Yeah, I know," I said.

"She doesn't talk bad about you, you know," Sam said.

I didn't respond. She came forward and sat down beside me.

"Kaity?" she asked.

"Yeah?"

She brushed my hair back and stared at me, her features stern.

"I think I love you."

I couldn't believe what I was hearing. This was all I had wanted. I felt whole. I smiled up at her. "I think I love you too."

She crawled into bed with me and pulled me into her arms. I felt so warm, so happy. I wanted to lie here forever. But when I awoke, Sam wasn't with me. I couldn't believe this was happening all over again. I searched the entire apartment and around the couch this time, too. But all for nothing.

The sun had gone down, and I had no way of contacting her. I assumed the worst, only stirred up more frustration. Maybe she had gone out with Laura again. Maybe they were out to get drugs. Who knew? I didn't. Nor was I going to find out, because Sam had made no effort whatsoever to leave me a note of any sort. Infuriated, I showered and jumped back into bed. I had to be up in a few hours—one of us had to work.

When I awoke again at six a.m., I prepared breakfast and packed a lunch. I felt sick to my stomach. Sam was still gone. What was I supposed to do? Call the police? I considered calling Laura, but I didn't know her number, and it was way too early in the morning. I threw my dishes into the sink and heard a glass shatter but didn't care. I was pissed. How had she been so thoughtless to leave me alone without informing me of her whereabouts?

Right when I grabbed the door handle to exit the apartment, keys rattled on the other side. I peered through the peephole and saw Sam's figure rocking from side to side. She could barely stand straight. I opened the door.

"Oh. Shit," she said, rolling her bloodshot eyes up at me.

"Shit?" I repeated. I wasn't sure what to say. Had she honestly just tried to sneak in?

"Scared me," she said and pushed me aside to walk into the apartment.

"What's wrong with you?" I asked.

"What do you mean?" she asked. She started opening and closing every cupboard in the kitchen.

"Where the hell were you last night?" I snapped.

"Out," she said simply.

"Where?" I asked. Now I was fuming.

"You're not my mom; give me a fucking break." She finally found a loaf of bread, opened the fridge, and stuck her head inside.

"Sam, where were you? With Laura?" I

continued.

She pulled out a few tomatoes and some mayonnaise. I knew that this conversation wasn't going anywhere. I wanted to swear at her—to call her every name in the book. But now wasn't the time. So I slammed the front door and went to work.

"Hey Maddi," I said, refusing to look at her.

"Hey," she said, "you okay?"

"Yeah."

And those were the only words we shared all day. I didn't say goodbye to her when I left. I wasn't sure why I was taking it out on her; she hadn't done anything wrong. I wondered if it had anything to do with her warning. Had she been right? Was I angry for not having listened?

I didn't go home that evening. Instead, I hopped onto a different bus and went to my parents' house. I wouldn't mention my problems. I just wanted to see my family. I hadn't spoken to them in a few weeks now.

I had completely forgotten it was supper time; when I walked in, my family and Andrew were gathered around the dinner table, fully engaged in conversation. I was about to turn around, not wanting to disrupt them, but Amy spotted me near the entryway.

"Kaity!" she shouted, and everyone's eyes turned on me.

Awkwardly, I removed my boots. "Hey,

guys..." There was no turning back now.

"Hey kid, come join us," my dad said.

He disappeared into the living room and returned with an extra chair. I sat down with them and mainly discussed my new job. I described how awesome Maddi was (or rather, how awesome she *had* been when I first met her). I was bitter now. Although I was happy to be with my family, all I wanted to do was swallow the bottle of red wine which was teasingly located at the very center of the table. I wanted to forget my problems. I wanted to be back in high school, back in my stage of denial. Things had been so much simpler.

"Thanks for supper guys," I said and hugged them each goodbye, including Andrew, before I left.

It looked as though he was going to be sticking around for a while longer, so I knew it was wisest to begin treating him as my brother-in-law. My mother insisted that I return soon and that she would bake my favorite meat pie for me next time.

I walked out into the cold and caught my bus just as it arrived. I wondered if Sam had been worrying about me. Would she be angry with me? I hoped so. This would prove to me that she cared. But when I arrived home, Sam wasn't there. The lights were all out, and the apartment was chilly. I somehow wished that

Maddi was with me, or even Matt. I didn't want to be alone. This place was so empty—so lifeless.

I made myself some Kraft Dinner and sat in front of the TV for the remainder of my night. By ten o'clock, Sam had still not returned. I would stay up all night waiting if I had to. I felt that familiar, awful anger rise in the back of my throat, and all I wanted to do was punch holes in the walls. So instead, I poured myself a screwdriver and swallowed it down in three gulps. By my fourth drink, my nerves had calmed.

I had completely forgotten that I was supposed to work the next day. But, it was too late now. I would simply have to call in sick. So I poured myself a fifth drink and changed the channel. I needed comedy. I felt so numb sitting there, my legs resting on the living room coffee table. The TV's bright lights illuminated the room, and the sound became hypnotizing. I felt so good right now, not caring about Sam's absence.

It was around one in the morning when I heard her struggling at the front door. I didn't bother to get up. I finished my drink and poured myself a fresh one, emptying the forty of vodka. Sam burst into the apartment and fell against the wall. She closed the door and walked into the kitchen. I heard her scavenging for food again, but I didn't help her, nor did I say hi.

She joined me in the living room with her tomato sandwich, sat down, and changed the channel. I stared at her as she cracked open a beer, and then I ripped the remote out of her hands and hit *last*. I was there first. We would watch what I was watching. But her eyes narrowed at the TV.

"I don't wanna watch this shit," was the first thing she said to me.

"I don't care; I'm watching it," I said. "You were gone, so it's my choice."

"Give me a break. I paid for the TV," she said.

She snatched the remote right out of my hand and browsed through the channels. I wanted to kick her. I wanted to throw my drink in her face. Why was she being so cruel to me? What had I done?

"What the hell's wrong with you?" I snapped.

"Don't you have to work tomorrow or something? Go to bed," she said, not once glancing my way. She pulled out a cigarette and lit it.

"Wow, you've been a real bitch lately. I should never have moved in with you," I said and went to bed.

I had hoped that this would shake her, that

she would chase me to either continue the fight or to apologize for her behavior. But she didn't. I heard her laugh in the living room as the TV echoed incomprehensible things. So I squeezed my eyes shut and cried myself to sleep.

Chapter 18

When I awoke in the morning, it came as no surprise that Sam was gone. My hangover wasn't as bad as I had expected, so I planned to still go to work. I forced myself out of bed and wiped my swollen eyes. I stared around the empty room for a few moments. How had things fallen apart so quickly? I thought she loved me. Who had Sam become? What happened to the striking Samantha Boward I first met in school? I wanted to find her, drag her back home, and get some answers.

I took a deep breath and reminded myself that anger wasn't going to solve anything. But it was so hard to stay calm, to stay rational, when all I wanted to do was slap her. I kicked some dirty clothes around the room and shoved a bunch of papers off of the dresser. I needed an answer: something, anything!

I forced open the closet door and pulled out

as much as I could. Books, papers, clothes, boxes, you name it. There had to be something she was hiding from me. A diary—anything!

There was something. I'm not sure why I hadn't seen it before. How had I been so blind to all of it? But when the evidence fell in front of my knees, I knew that it was about time I opened my eyes. There were a bunch of them; blue, pink, and white pills. I had no idea what they were. To this day, I still don't know. They were all different shapes and sizes, wrapped safely in an old and worn-out Ziploc bag. I squeezed it tight and clenched my jaw. I almost went to throw them in the toilet, but I knew that this wasn't an intelligent thing to do. What was the point? She would buy more, and I would be yelled at, if not beaten.

So I got ready for work and hopped on the bus. The moment I stepped through Lacey's doors, I marched straight towards Maddi. Her large eyes must have known something was up because she didn't speak. She just watched me.

"You were right," I said and bit my lip. I wasn't going to cry. Not now. Not again. I felt my throat swell up, and I swallowed hard.

"Oh honey," Maddi said. She started forward, but I backed away. I didn't want a hug. It would only weaken me further.

"It's okay," I said. "I'm sorry I didn't believe you. I should've listened... What do I do now?"

Her blue eyes were so sympathetic, so understanding of my pain.

"Sweetheart, you have to get out of there. Leave, as soon as you can," she said.

"And what? I don't want to go back to my parents' place." I dropped my bag to the floor and sat on the bench behind the counter. "This is messed up. I knew she drank a lot, but drugs? I don't understand..." I swallowed hard and added, "she's just not the type."

Maddi squeezed my shoulder.

"I know it's hard, sweetheart, but it does get better, I promise. Why don't you stay with me for a while? I mean, maybe Sam will smarten up. Maybe losing you will jolt her out of it. Besides, my roommate moved out."

I looked up at her. Maybe this was my way out. What other choice did I have? I was living with an addict. There was no rationalizing with her. She wouldn't listen. I had to take action.

"I'm serious," Maddi persisted.

"But I don't want to imp..." I started.

"Kaity, you're not imposing. It's a win-win. As long as you don't mind helping out with the rent, that is," she said.

"Of course I don't mind!" I said. "I mean, like, well, when?" I stuttered.

I was overwhelmed. It seemed as though only yesterday, Sam and I were happily apartment-hunting together. And now, I didn't know who she was anymore, but I knew I had to leave her. She wasn't the Sam I knew.

"Whenever you're ready," Maddi said.

I didn't give Maddi any of the messy details. I figured that Sam's problem was private, and although I was extremely angry, I didn't want to make Sam look like a monster. I loved her, regardless of everything she was putting me through.

So the moment I got home, I started packing. I used plastic bags for laundry and my school bag for a few important things such as my mp3 player, my makeup, my phone, and my wallet. Everything else belonged to Sam. I considered walking out now and leaving a note behind, but I couldn't do it. I had to see her face. I had to witness her reaction to my decision, the consequence of her actions.

So I stewed on the couch, grinding my teeth. My stomach felt as though someone had tied it into several knots. I was so anxious, so afraid of her reaction. But I had to do this. When I finally heard her keys at the door, my heart raced. Should I go through with it? I wondered. Maybe a talk would suffice. No, it wouldn't. She was too far gone. I had to put my foot down. Threats were not going to do anything.

The moment she walked in, my anger was replaced with shock. She stumbled in laughing with Laura behind her. And what had she done to her hair? The black had been replaced by a maroon red, and it was cut into layers, giving it a shaggier appearance. It was nice, but I shook away my attraction to her and focused on the situation at hand.

"Oh. Hey," she said when she saw me.

I didn't respond. Instead, I sat there, unable to speak. I was terrified. She walked towards me, and I flinched when she leaned in for a kiss. Would she hurt me? Why was I so scared of her? She lit a smoke and threw her lighter on the table. But as she did so, I noticed a dark design around her wrist. The dark colors were decorated by a pinkish swelling. A tattoo.

I stood up and grabbed her arm tightly. Her red, lazy eyes looked up at me and she smiled.

"Rough. I like it," she said.

"When did you get this?" I asked, looking down at her arm. The tattoo was of two black snakes, intertwining themselves around her wrist.

"Get what?" she asked. She was so out of it—so absent from reality.

"This," I said more loudly, and I raised her arm so she could see it herself.

She glared down at it and jerked her head backward in surprise.

"Huh," she said.

"Huh?" I repeated.

Laura laughed in the background, and Sam joined in.

"What's so funny?" I asked, my tone hardening.

"I don't remember getting this done," Sam said and burst into uncontrollable laughter.

Laura too, was now cramped over, and she was pointing at Sam, accusing her of being *crazy*. I didn't find this funny in the slightest. I pushed her arm away and walked into the bedroom. I grabbed my bags, and then the little sack of pills I had found earlier that morning. I was so angry that I didn't understand how I was still standing. My legs were shaking, and I could barely hold my bags. I walked back out to a bunch of laughing hyenas and threw the bag of pills at Sam's face.

The laughter stopped so suddenly that I retreated into myself and wondered if I had made a grave mistake. Sam looked down at the bag and stiffened. I swallowed hard and took a step back. Her head rocked forward, but then straightened. She was so out of it. Was she going to hurt me? All I wanted to do was run, but I couldn't. I couldn't speak; I couldn't move. I stared at her narrowing green eyes, and I wanted to throw up.

"Where did you find these?" she asked. Her eyes were locked on me.

"In... Um—" I said.

I couldn't answer. What the hell was wrong with me? She looked so enraged, so deathly.

"Where the fuck did you find these?" She took a step toward me.

I nearly fell back, but I caught myself against the wall. This had been a mistake; it was clear to me now. Why had I done that? Laura was staring wide-eyed at both of us.

"You think you can just go snooping around people's things like that?" Sam shouted.

I thought I would faint. I felt my heart thumping against my ribs, and I knew that there was no escape. She walked forward with determination and grabbed me by the collar of my shirt. She was so strong, and I felt so weak. She shook me hard, and I felt the back of my head smash against the wall.

"Sam, please stop it. Please," I begged, my voice cracking.

"You're not fair. Why should I be fair?" she asked, and she shook me again. She pinned me hard against the wall and wrapped her fingers around my throat.

"Were you going to sell them? Is that it?" she said.

I tried to speak, but her fingers were wrapped too tightly. She smashed her closed fist against the side of my head, right above my temple, before letting me drop to the floor. My brain shook and my vision went blurry. My head throbbed, and my lower lip began to tremble.

"WELL?" she snapped, looking down at me as a lion would its prey.

"No. No. I wasn't. I swear. I only wanted you to stop. I love you. Sam, please," I cried.

"You're pathetic," she said and kicked me over.

I fell to my side and crawled up onto my hands and knees. What was I supposed to do now? I had no anger left in me. The sick part is that I wanted to hug her—to be held even though she was the one who was hurting me. I just wanted her love.

I slowly stood and picked up my bags.

"I know you didn't mean to hurt me, and I still love you," I said, wiping my eyes, "but I'm leaving. I can't have you treating me like this all the time."

I was so proud of myself for having spoken those words. It was as though someone, or something, had given me the necessary inner strength to defend myself against her demons.

"Leaving?" She walked towards me again. I stood straight and didn't back away this time.

"Yeah. I'm sorry," I said.

Her eyes were so cold. I could no longer see any form of love in them. And before I could say anything else, she slapped me across the face again. I felt my skin heat up and tingle. I didn't

hit her back. I looked away and waited for her
to say something.

"Then leave," she said.

And I did exactly that.

ONE MONTH LATER

I cried myself to sleep every night, trying to decipher how everything had fallen apart so unexpectedly.

I wondered if maybe this had all been some big misunderstanding, but Maddi forced me to see the truth.

I quit my job at Lacey's and spent my days around wine bottles, phone in hand.

She didn't call me.

TWO MONTHS LATER

The crying became intermittent, but deep down, I still hoped for that one phone call.

The temptation to go see her remained, even though I knew we wouldn't work.

Maddi explained to me that Sam was sick and that I could not cure her.

I repeated Maddi's words over and over again, hoping that this would ease the pain.

It didn't.

THREE MONTHS LATER

I finally understood Maddi's words. I wasn't Sam's savior.

I slowed my alcohol consumption when I realized I was destroying my body.

I still hoped to see her, but I realized that this would probably never happen again.

I was hired as a full-time receptionist at a very fancy hotel.

I swallowed my feelings.

Chapter 19

"No, I love that song. Leave it on!" Maddi yelled.

I glanced back at her and smirked. All right, I would leave it on this time. "Wonderwall," by Oasis. I loved this song too, but knowing that it was Maddi's favorite song, I always found a little amusement in denying her the freedom to listen to it.

I sipped my gin and tonic, even though I hated gin. But hey, we had received the bottle as a gift, so there wasn't going to be any waste. That night was all about celebration.

"To your new job," Maddi said, extending her glass.

"To your new crush," I said and stuck my tongue out at her.

"Damn right." She chugged the remainder of her drink. "But tonight, we're finding you one, too."

I rolled my eyes and smiled. Did I want to go

out to meet a new girl? Yes and no. I wanted Sam, as pathetic as I was being. I realized how irrational this desire was, but I had seen a part of Sam that no one else had: a sweet, loving side. That part of her was gone, though. And if I was going to forget about this torment, I would have to distract myself with lust.

"Maybe if we find you someone, we can go on a double date tomorrow!" Maddi said.

She was so excited, it was cute. And I swore to myself that if this guy was only in it for her body, I would personally track him down and beat him so hard that he could be strapped to a pole and mistaken for a flag at Pride.

"Maybe," I said, not wanting to comment any more than I had to.

"So have you been to The Palace yet?" she asked.

I shook my head. The only gay club I had ever entered was Taylor's Tower, or at least this was the only one I could remember having entered. There were things I didn't want to remember: Sam's excited face; the way she would kiss me; how protective she was of me; those guys at the end of the night; her beaten face.

"You okay?" Maddi asked.

"Huh?" I glanced up and realized that she had been staring at me. "I'm fine," I said.

"Look, stop thinking, okay? We'll have fun

212

tonight," she said.

I hoped it was true. I also hoped that I would run into Sam and that she would beg for my forgiveness. In a perfect world, this would happen. No. In a perfect world, Sam would never have let everything get so out of hand.

I threw on my makeup and swallowed my irrational feelings. To be quite honest, I wasn't excited as I stared out of the cab's window, analyzing every detail of the late, downtown life. The lights were blinding, and there were people everywhere. Road regulations may have as well been placed on hold; people didn't seem to care about road signs. The cab driver drove aggressively, but I had confidence in him. When we finally arrived at one of the busiest streets of downtown Loshano, Maddi signaled the cab driver to pull over and handed him a twenty.

"Thanks," she said and hopped out.

I followed close behind, wondering how it was that Maddi knew everything about downtown.

"So," I said, glancing up at the two-story Palace, "this is a gay club?"

I looked around for more clues but couldn't quite fit the puzzle pieces together. Although my memory was a little hazy due to drunkenness, I was still able to conclude that this wasn't the gay village of downtown. I didn't see rainbows anywhere, and most couples were heterosexual.

"You're cute," Maddi said.

I gawked at her and asked, "Where are we?"

"This isn't a gay club, but it's gay every first Friday of the month." She grabbed my hand and said, "Come on."

I scanned my surroundings once again, and part of me wished that Sam was there to see me holding Maddi's hand. I wanted her to be jealous and to regret everything she'd done to me.

When we entered, it wasn't at all what I had expected. It looked very chic. There were glass tables everywhere, and the floors were cleaner than my shoes. The gay men were dressed to the nines, and I suddenly became quite uncomfortable. I looked down at my jeans and sneakers and wondered if perhaps I had underdressed. But I spotted a few other casuals as we walked across the dance floor, and I realized that I wasn't half-bad looking.

I felt my heart pump faster when I noticed a group of girls staring my way, whispering among one another. Were they laughing at me? Or were they checking me out? This wasn't high school—they were most definitely checking me out. I felt my lips curve into a smile, and my posture straightened. It felt good.

"Wow, you're already being assessed."

Maddi nudged me in the ribs.

I laughed and walked to the bar with her. We ordered beers, and I couldn't help but notice more and more girls glancing back at me now and then. For the first time in a long time, I wasn't thinking about Sam. I was receiving a confidence boost, and I was loving every second of it.

"Looks like you're fresh meat," Maddi said, leaning in. She turned back to face the bar. "Two vodkas please."

"Nah, they're probably checking you out," I said in her ear, trying to fake modesty. But I knew very well that their eyes were on me.

"Please, Kaity. They know I'm not gay. It's called gaydar; you should go buy it at Walmart," she yelled over the music.

"What's gaydar? Is it expensive?" I asked.

Maddi's jaw dropped and she burst into hysterical laughter. I leaned in to hear what the joke was all about, but the loud bass made it difficult. She handed me a vodka shot and *cheersed* me. It was disgusting, but it refreshed my insides.

"You're one of a kind," she said, shaking her head.

I didn't get it, so I drank my beer and scanned the multicolored room. I froze on the spot when a young, blonde-haired woman approached me. She had medium-length hair and appeared to be pretty drunk.

"Hey there," she said.

I looked at Maddi, fearful, then back at the woman.

"Hey," I said.

"My friend thinks you're real cute," she said and glanced back over her shoulder.

I followed her eyes and spotted another woman leaning against the wall with a drink in her hand. She was staring intensely my way, a smirk on her lips. I hesitated. I had never done this before.

"I think she's really pretty, too," I said and smiled stupidly.

I could barely see what the other woman looked like, but I knew this was the polite response.

"What's your name?" she asked.

"Um, Kaity. You?"

"Come," the blonde girl said, ignoring my question altogether. She grabbed my hand, and I reached for Maddi's so I wouldn't lose her.

We walked across the room to meet the woman's friend.

"Kaity, this is Briana. Briana, Kaity." And with that, the blonde woman walked away.

This was so awkward. I looked around nervously and then stretched an open hand to greet her.

"Hey Kaity," Briana said, "I'm sorry about

that. My friend has a big mouth and she really enjoys embarrassing me."

I couldn't help but laugh. I turned around to find Maddi, but she had left us, too.

"Can I buy you a drink?" she asked, raising an eyebrow.

I looked down at my half-empty beer and shrugged.

"Sure," I said and smiled at her.

It was so difficult to carry on a conversation due to the music. I was guessing every other spoken word. We headed over to the bar, and Briana ordered me another Bud. I thanked her and clanged the neck of her beer with mine.

She had dark hair and honey-brown eyes, and her skin was of a darker shade. I couldn't quite figure out her ethnicity. She was stunning. Her dark eyes were on me, staring intensely. It made me uncomfortable, but I knew it was best to behave nonchalantly. Maybe this *intensity* was normal in gay clubs. I smiled awkwardly again and scanned the room, acting as though I was busy looking for someone.

"So, you seeing anyone?" she asked.

Wow, right to the point. I couldn't believe it. I hesitated and thought about Sam. Why had she reminded me? Ugh. But, I wasn't seeing Sam. I hadn't been with Sam for months now, and there was no point allowing a past relationship to sabotage a potential future romance.

"No, no I'm not. You?" I asked.

"Well I wouldn't be here if I were, silly," she said, narrowing her eyes on me.

It made me nervous, but I enjoyed the feeling. I didn't say anything and just smiled back.

"You're gorgeous; I hope you know that. I'm sorry if that's a little direct," she said and sipped her beer.

"Oh. Um. Thanks. You too," I said. Why was I being so dull? Why was this so difficult?

"You don't go out much, do you?" she laughed.

"That obvious, huh?" I asked.

"A little."

We both chuckled, and the alcohol finally started to take effect on me. I became more relaxed, more confident about myself.

"Wanna sit?" she asked.

"Sure," I said.

She grabbed my wrist and led me to the seating area. It was much quieter in comparison to the dance floor.

"First time in here?" she asked once we finally sat down.

I nodded. "It's nice," I said, "and you?"

"Nah, I come a lot. I have no life, so, ya know," she said.

She had a pretty face, and her personality only embellished it further. I tried to imagine what it would feel like to kiss her. I had never kissed anyone else but Sam. How different would it be? Would her lips be a different texture? Or were all lips relatively alike?

I suddenly returned to reality and noticed her eyes were scanning my face—my eyes, my lips, my eyes again. Was she thinking the same thing? I hadn't had the time to analyze the situation any further; she leaned in slowly, resting her hand on my thigh. And although I had wondered what her lips would feel like, I couldn't follow through with the idea in the physical world. I turned my head to the side and her lips pressed up against my cheek.

"Oh. I'm sorry," she said, somewhat taken aback.

I felt like an idiot for being so rude. This beautiful girl had tried to kiss me, and I had refused her. Why? This was my chance to forget Sam.

"Too soon; I get it," she said and nodded, clearly embarrassed.

"No, I'm sorry," I said. "I..."

She looked up at me, her eyes desperately awaiting an explanation.

"I'm in love with someone, and I don't want to kiss anyone else," I said.

I bowed my head and looked down at my

hands. I wasn't sure why I was being so open with her, but I knew it was for the best. Perhaps it was my drunkenness, perhaps not; but it didn't matter. It was the truth. I was still in love with Sam.

"Ahh," she said and tilted her head back, "I get it, really. An ex, huh?" she asked.

I nodded.

"Don't worry about it, it takes time. Trust me, I've been through it more than once." She rolled her eyes.

I forced a laugh. At least I wasn't alone.

"How long does it take?" I asked.

"It depends. Everyone's different. I wish I could help ya out."

"Thanks," I said. "I'm sure it'll be fine," and I chugged the remainder of my beer. "Can I buy you one now?" I asked.

She smirked at me and nodded.

Chapter 20

I woke up and stared at the ceiling. Was I home? At Maddi's? I quickly glanced around. I was in my room (Maddi's house). I recollected last night's events and suddenly remembered Briana. I smiled at the memory of our conversations, and how well we had gotten along.

I rolled over and stretched my arms, but to my surprise, I hit something hard. I pushed aside some pillows and spotted my phone. Uh oh. Had I called someone? Why couldn't I remember? How much had I had to drink? I was always blacking out; I didn't understand why I couldn't control myself. I exhaled a deep breath and grabbed my phone. *Please, please, please,* I begged mentally, hoping that I hadn't done what I had promised myself to never do. But then I suddenly remembered that Sam no longer had a cell phone. How could I have contacted her?

I opened up my phone and checked my most recent calls. There was a phone number I didn't recognize, and I wondered if Sam had called me. I checked my text messages. This unfamiliar number was there again, with a new message time-stamped from this morning. I opened it up:

"It gets easier, don't worry."

Briana. She was the one I had talked to late last night over the phone. Had I whined about my feelings for Sam? Was this what she was referring to? I checked my last call time: twenty-three minutes. Shit. What the hell had we talked about for twenty-three minutes? I considered texting her back, but I was too embarrassed now. What would I say? *Hey, I don't remember what we talked about, but thanks for the chat.* Yeah, right.

I rolled out of bed and dragged myself into the kitchen. I needed food. Anything to cure this hangover.

"Well, well, well..." Maddi said.

My puffy eyes followed her voice and I found her seated at the kitchen table, a coffee in one hand, the paper in the other.

"Good morning, sunshine," she said.

"Hah," I said and opened the fridge door.

"You're lucky I live with you," she said and sipped her coffee.

"How do you figure?" I pulled a plate of leftover lasagna from the fridge.

"I don't think you would have made it home without me," she said with a laugh.

"That drunk, huh?" I asked, not wanting to hear the answer.

"Mhm. But on the bright side, you got a girl's phone number."

"Briana?" I asked.

"I don't know. The pretty, exotic-looking one," she said and returned to her paper.

Yeah, Briana. Well, I *had* gotten her number. Had I been sober, I would have probably shied away from the conversation.

"So, you still going on a date with Norman?" I asked.

"Nathan," Maddi corrected. "Yeppers, tonight at eight. He's taking me to some restaurant. It's a surprise, so I have no clue where it is!"

She was so excited. I was sincerely happy for her.

"That's awesome," I said and took a bite of cold, leftover lasagna. It was so much better this way—unheated.

"I know, isn't it? Hey, why don't you get Briana to come here while I'm gone? You guys should hang out."

"Um, I barely know her."

"So? Have a few drinks; you'll loosen up."

I pondered this idea for a few seconds but then decided against it. It would be weird. Besides, I had told her that I was in love with Sam. How much weirder could things get? She would come here for what? To talk about it? I was certain I had talked her ear off last night about my pathetic heartbreak.

"Nah, I don't think so," I said.

Maddi shrugged. "Your call. Still think it would do you some good."

I left it at that and went into the living room to watch some TV. I realized I had been watching TV for nearly six hours when I saw Maddi pop out into the living room, wearing a forest-green dress. It was stunning.

"How do I look?" she asked, twirling in circles.

I smiled.

"You look great, Maddi."

"Thanks." She grinned and skipped back to her bedroom to complete her hair and makeup process.

I stared towards the kitchen and wondered if one beer would be so bad. It was only one, and besides, it would help me with my hangover, as Sam had taught me. So I obeyed my conscience and found myself reaching for a cold one in the fridge.

"He's here. Wish me luck!" Maddi ran to the front door, her arms waving in the air with excitement.

Three beers later I found myself flipping my phone open and scanning through the few phone numbers I had. Would it really be so bad to invite her over? I mean, it wasn't fair. Everyone else had romance in their lives; why couldn't I?

Okay, so I didn't want romance. But I did enjoy the attention. It was nice, what can I say? It felt great to feel wanted again. I swallowed hard and created a new message,

"Hey, sorry about my drunken whining. If you wanna watch a movie or something tonight, let me know."

I took a deep breath, found Briana's number, and hit send.

BEED-A-LEEP.

The sound of my phone caused my heart muscles to clench. I chugged the remainder of my beer and opened my phone, afraid of what the message might read.

"Ya sounds great. Ten okay? I dont kno where u live."

No way! She had accepted! To be honest, I was more excited about the fact that I now had plans. It didn't so much matter that they were with Briana; I wasn't looking for romance. I didn't feel any sort of lust towards her, no matter how beautiful she was. I somehow felt guilty for having invited her over since I knew that she wanted more. But that wasn't my concern, I told myself. I'd been upfront with her. So I sent her my address and had another beer.

My shoulders jerked forward when I heard the doorbell ring. I pressed pause on *The Ring* and stood up. Although the movie was terrifying, I was more focused on the black-haired character. I wondered if Sam could have pulled off the look, had she wet her hair and thrown it over her face. I opened the door. The big grin on Briana's face proved to me that she didn't think of this as a "just-friends" night. I suddenly wondered if this had been a bad idea.

"How's it going?" she asked and walked in. She was carrying a little six-pack of fruity coolers, so I grabbed them for her as any gentleman would have done.

"Here. I'll put those in the fridge for you. And I'm good; how're you?" I asked.

"Doing good." Her gaze lingered on me.

It made me uncomfortable, but at the same time, it was flattering. I placed her drinks in the kitchen fridge and cracked one of her bottles open for her.

"Here," I said.

She grabbed it. "Thanks. What're you watching?"

"The Ring."

"Oh no way, I love this movie." She plopped

down onto the couch.

I wondered if she actually liked the movie or if she was only saying that to make me happy—to make it appear as though we had something in common. She would have probably said the same thing had I been watching *The Lion King* or some kid's Disney movie. Don't get me wrong, I'm a huge fan of Disney!

I sat down beside her, feeling a little awkward. Even though I was no longer with Sam, it seemed like cheating. I felt as though Sam would walk into the room at any moment now and would wonder who this Briana was. I shook those thoughts away and focused on my movie.

"So why aren't you out partying? It's Saturday night," Briana said, glancing my way.

I shrugged. "I guess I did enough partying last night."

"Yeah, know what you mean," she laughed. "I'm pretty beat myself."

I smiled at her, not knowing what else to say. Ugh, this was horrible. Why had I invited her here? I chugged the rest of my beer and went into the kitchen to make myself a strong rum and Coke. Surely, this would help.

Halfway through my drink, I was finally beginning to relax. I didn't seem to care so much what Briana thought anymore, nor was I afraid to say something silly. But one thing was for sure—I wasn't going to bring up Sam.

"How long did you and your ex date? If you don't mind my asking," she said

Hah. Hey, I wasn't the one who brought it up.

"Um, a few months, I guess," I said, realizing how silly it sounded. After all of my blabbering, she had probably expected to hear something more along the lines of *four years*.

"Oh."

Yep, it had taken her by surprise.

"I know it isn't long, but I don't know. She was intense. Anyways, it's not a good topic for tonight," I said and tried my best to stretch out a warm smile.

"Yeah all right," she said. "Hey, do you like Skittles?"

"Not so much; they hurt my teeth."

She chuckled and shook her head. Apparently, I'd missed the punchline.

"I meant the drug."

My eyes went wide and I grinned at her.

"I didn't know Skittles were a drug. I thought they were candy," I said, feeling like such a moron.

"E," she said.

"What?"

She rolled her eyes and laughed again. She reached into her pocket and pulled out a Ziploc bag filled with tiny pills.

"Ecstasy," she said.

And my heart sank. I stared at her open palm and felt my jaw clench. The room went around my head a few times, and I remembered kneeling in my room, Sam's pill pouch resting delicately at the tips of my fingers. I remembered having thrown the bag at her, and how she had pinned me up against the wall. I remembered her warm, intoxicated breath brushing up against the lining of my jaw and how I had known that this person was no longer Sam.

"You okay?" Briana asked. She slowly slid the bag back into her pocket. I didn't have to say anything. She clearly understood that I wasn't a fan. "Hey man, I'm sorry. I shouldn't have asked."

I allowed my wide eyes to relax and looked away and sipped my drink.

"It's all good," I said.

Deep breaths. Deep breaths. Briana wasn't Sam, and it wasn't her fault that Sam had fallen into such a destructive path. I repeated this to myself, while Briana remained silent. I looked over at her. I could tell she was ashamed, so I smiled at her.

"Hey listen, not your fault. I'm not a fan," I explained.

"Yeah, that's cool. I don't blame you," she said and shrugged.

I stared at her a little longer than I had hoped.

"You do it often?" I asked.

"No, actually. I've only done it once or twice. Everyone I know seems to be doing it, so I thought I would impress you if I had some available. I know it's stupid, and I'm so sorry."

All right. Even though I had nearly wanted to strangle her, her reason was kind of cute. So she wasn't a drug addict, but she had assumed that I would want some. Or had she assumed that I was a druggy? Now I wasn't too sure whether this had been cute or was a blatant insult.

"Do I look like a druggy to you?" I asked.

"No! No! Not at all!" she blurted. She was so nervous now. This was so unlike the first impression I'd had of her. "It's... it's a lot of people in the clubs. I don't know. Look, I'm sorry," she said.

"It's okay," I said and laughed. "I'm only teasing."

She looked up at me and smirked, her eyes narrowing.

"Funny," she said and nudged me over. I laughed and nudged her back.

"Yeah, thanks for noticing," I said. "I should start my own stand-up comedy show."

And although I had rejected her last night, I didn't turn away when she leaned in this time.

Her smooth, rose-colored lips pressed up against mine, and I accepted it. She was so warm, so affectionate. Sam's lips had always felt dangerous and exciting. I couldn't even begin to compare the two, as this was entirely new to me. My second kiss. All of these thoughts combined caused me to pull away without a word.

"You okay?" she asked.

"Yeah. I'm sorry. Thanks."

"You're welcome," she said, her smile returning.

And I realized that I too, was smiling. Had I enjoyed it? Did I like Briana without even knowing it? I was so confused. We returned to our movie in silence. As Briana's attention was entirely focused on a specific scene, I glanced over at her and observed the TV's colorful glow, as it accentuated different parts of her face. I wondered if perhaps we stood a chance and if I could ever love her. I looked away before she caught me staring and went to make myself another drink.

I nearly fell into the cupboards when I entered the kitchen, and that's when I realized I was drunk. Surely these feelings I thought I had for Briana were nothing more than drunken loneliness. Did I need another drink? No. But, I made one anyhow and brought her another cooler.

Chapter 21

"Kaityyyy," came a whiny voice.

I cracked open my eyes and found Maddi sitting at the end of my bed.

"What?" I moaned.

"You've been sleeping all day! It's five o'clock. Get your lazy ass up!" she said.

"Mmm," I mumbled. Ugh. I was so tired, so weak.

"I want to know how it went last night, and I'll tell you how my date went. Come on, come on, come on!"

Why did she have to be so loud? The vein in my forehead pulsated and I threw my pillow over my head. But it didn't help. Her hand reached under my blanket and tickled my side. I jerked away and laughed forcefully, when all I wanted to do was strangle her. Now wasn't a good time. I was so nauseous.

"Kaity? Come on. Did you and Briana, well,

kiss or anything?"

Briana! How had Maddi known? I had told her I wasn't going to invite Briana. I removed the pillow from my face and looked down at her.

"How did you know she was here?" I asked, my voice hoarser than ever.

"You guys fell asleep on the couch together. I don't know how you made it back into your bed." She shrugged.

Great.

"What do you mean 'together'? On separate sides, I hope," I said.

"Um, I don't know, it was dark. Think you were laying your head on her lap though," she said.

I moaned. This was technically considered cuddling.

"She left this morning. I gave her toast for breakfast." Maddi said.

I didn't respond.

"Well, aren't you gonna ask me about my date?" she asked.

"Oh yeah," I said, "how was Nor... Nathan? Did you guys *kiss*?" I asked, emphasizing the kiss word with such a mocking tone that she laughed and smacked my shoulder.

"Actually no. He wanted to, but I didn't let him. Gives me control; I like it," she said, grinning.

"Smart," I said.

"I know. So we're going out again next Friday. He's really sweet," she said.

I could tell she was happy. Her cheeks were all rosy and her eyes glowed.

"That's awesome Maddi." And I meant it.

"I know," she said and jumped off my bed.

"I'm making macaroni salad if you're hungry," she said before disappearing.

Right now, food did not sound appetizing to me whatsoever. But I knew that I would eat later. Maddi made the most flavorsome macaroni salad I had ever tasted. I rolled over and closed my eyes. The next day would be my big day—my first day of work at the Loshano Inn hotel. Was I looking forward to it? Yes, and no. I hadn't worked in so long, I worried it would be overwhelming. But hey, I had to pick myself up and move on. I had a life to live.

I spent the remainder of my Sunday curing my hangover. It was a slow, painful process, but it had to be done. I needed a clear head for work the next day. I'd had enough. It was time to sober up and to stop moping around. I had a great job lined up and a girl who liked me. What did I have to whine about? Nothing. Later that night, I prepared myself lunch with Maddi's leftover macaroni salad and set out my work clothes for the next day.

Morning arrived much sooner than I had

hoped. I grabbed my things, shuffled down a quick bowl of cereal, and made my way to the bus stop. Deep breaths and head held high, I reminded myself.

When I arrived at the Loshano Inn, I tilted my head back to analyze the twenty-story building. The glass windows were spotless, and the stairs were shining brighter than any car in my line of sight. For twenty dollars an hour as a receptionist, you can imagine how well this place did. I watched as high-class businesspeople entered and exited the huge, golden-rimmed doors, and I wondered what I had gotten myself into. Was I underdressed? I looked down at my black dress pants and white blouse. Surely this would be acceptable.

I raised my chin and walked on ahead. But of course, my first impression had to be ruined by some petty, unusual happening. I hadn't had the time to hop out of the way when an old woman dropped her oversized purse right in front of my feet. My foot caught in the leather strap and I dove forward. It was like a slow-motion movie clip. My arms swung in the air, and I ran forward and up the stairs in an attempt to regain composure, but this did not save me.

I heard a few gasps. My face crashed against the cold edge of a stair and everything went black. When I opened my eyes again, many well-dressed men were crouching around me.

"Are you all right, young lady?" one of them asked.

A droplet of blood slid down the curve of my right eyebrow and into my eye. Great. My first day at work, and I was showing up with a bloody face. I wiped the mess and sat up straight.

"I'm okay," I said.

And I was. I mean, I could feel my forehead throbbing, but that was nothing in comparison to my embarrassment. I smiled at each one of them and continued my path towards the front doors. There were a few shocked whispers shared among the crowd as I walked away, and all I wanted to do was vanish into oblivion. But no, I had to walk up those stupid stairs, eyes aimed at the back of my head.

Right as I walked in, the concierge was the first person to speak.

"Goodness!" he said.

He was a handsome, young-looking Latino man. He stood up and rushed around his desk to my aid.

"It's okay," I said and shook my head.

"Okay?" he laughed. "You look as though someone threw a tomato at your face. I apologize if that is vulgar," he said. His accent was adorable. He seemed so innocent and warmhearted.

"Not vulgar, honest," I said and smiled at him.

"Come with me." He motioned me to follow him.

"I'm supposed to be here at eight. I'm going to be late if I go clean this up," I said, hesitating to follow.

"Nonsense. I will explain to Charlene what has happened," he said, and continued along.

Charlene. Yes, that name sounded familiar. She was the woman who would train me. Well, surely the concierge knew what he was talking about. I wouldn't get into trouble over an accident. So I followed him as he brought me into a small lounge with a door labeled "STAFF" in large letters. The room was as beautiful as any other area of the hotel. I'd been given a tour when I came in for my interview—an interview obtained through the Internet, might I add. Gotta love technology.

"Here, sit," he said and pointed at a black leather chair.

I did as told and observed him as he searched through a few cabinets, mumbling incomprehensible things to himself.

"Aha!" he said and pulled out a small first-aid kit. "This may sting a little, but is for your own good," he said.

I squinted and held my breath as he cleaned my face. He spread a layer of ointment over the wound and covered it with a transparent Band-Aid.

"You're pretty good at this," I said.

"Practice make perfect." He grabbed my face and smirked. "Good as new!"

"Thanks... Antonio," I said, glancing down at his name tag.

"You are most welcome..." he said, staring at me.

"Kaitlyn. Or Kaity, whichever," I said.

"I like Kaitlyn."

"All right, you can call me Kaitlyn," I said.

"So, today is first day, yes?" he asked.

"Yeah," I said. "I'm kinda nervous."

"No. Do not be nervous. Charlene is very nice," he said. "Come, you may meet her."

I followed him back into the lobby, where two receptionists were lined up behind a high, dark green marble counter. The one on the right looked up as we arrived.

"Charlene, Kaitlyn had a fall. Forgive her timing; it is my fault," Antonio said.

"Yeah yeah, it's always your fault, isn't it?" she said and stuck out her tongue. "Hi there Kaitlyn, I'm Charlene." She rose from behind the counter and stretched her arm in my direction.

"Hey Charlene, you can call me Kaity," I said, shaking her hand.

"Holy! Talk about a good first day, eh?" she

said, staring at my forehead.

I laughed and rubbed my Band-Aid.

"Yeah, I know. Those damned purses can be deadly," I said.

At this, she giggled and said, "I like you already, Kaity. Come on over, let's get started."

I spent all afternoon learning how to use the computer system, how to book reservations, and how to process payments. She made me take my first call after a few hours of observation, and I nearly wet myself. I was so nervous—so afraid to mess up. But I didn't—I did pretty well.

"Psst. If Charlene here gives you a hard time, smack her a good one," said the other woman beside me.

I wasn't sure whether to laugh at her comment or not. I smiled at her, and she extended her hand to clear the awkwardness.

"I'm Gloria," she said sweetly.

I shook her hand and introduced myself. Everyone there was so friendly. Gloria must have been in her late sixties and Charlene in her mid-thirties. I felt out of place physically, but psychologically, I felt more comfortable around these people than I had ever felt around anyone in high school. I listened carefully as Charlene went on about her six-year-old son and how much trouble it was to raise a child. She had such a strong personality—the type I seemed to subconsciously attract.

I laughed when Gloria stepped in. "Oh stop your whining Charlene. You just wait till that kid hits sixteen; then you'll wish he was six again."

Gloria obviously knew what she was talking about. Surely she had had kids before, and most likely, grandchildren.

"What about you, dear?" Gloria asked.

"Hmm?" I said.

"Got any kids?"

"Hell no" was what I nearly blurted, but instead, I smiled at her and shook my head.

"Plan on having any?" she asked.

"I don't think so."

"Good, don't. Trust me," Charlene said, resting a hand on my arm, "they take your life away."

"Oh stop it," Gloria said, frowning at Charlene. "Sweetheart, they're little gifts. You gotta take the good with the bad," she said.

"Don't listen to Granny here," Charlene said and winked at Gloria.

They both laughed and Gloria went on to answer her phone, "Thank you for calling Loshano Inn. Gloria speaking; how may I help you today?"

These two women were awesome. They were so friendly, easygoing, and humorous. No way would I have a bad time at work. This was fresh entertainment. I was so happy when I went home. Maddi was sitting in the living room with some guy, and I told her everything that had happened. After babbling on for nearly ten minutes, I realized this poor guy was just sitting there, listening to me rant.

"Wow, I'm sorry. I'm Kaity, by the way," I said and chuckled.

"Hey," he said, laughing, "it's all good. I'm Nathan."

Aha. *The* Nathan. Good job, Maddi. This boy was pretty cute, in a rugged sort of way. I smirked at Maddi on my way out, and I knew that she knew precisely what I was thinking. I rushed into my bedroom, wanting nothing more than to text Sam about the great day I had just had. But of course, I couldn't do that. I had to stop thinking that she was still a part of my life. This sudden realization sucked all the joy right out of me, and I began to feel sluggish and depressed. I dropped onto my bed and flipped my phone open.

1 New Message from Briana. This changed my tune. I smiled. I opened the message, which read:

"Hey! How was ur first day?"

My happiness returned. How had I forgotten about Briana? This was the sweetest thing she could have done—asked me how my day had gone. Sam probably wasn't even thinking about me right now. Why was I wasting my thoughts on her, when I had just met this wonderful girl who couldn't stop thinking about me?

I replied,

"Great! Thanks. Come see me?"

I wanted her here. I wanted to see that familiar smile on her face, the way she looked at me as if I were a goddess without flaw. Although I didn't yet know her very well, she made me strangely comfortable.

"Be there in thirty," she responded.

Yes! I rushed into the kitchen and prepared some Kraft Dinner. As the noodles thickened and a creamy odor filled my nostrils, the doorbell rang. Perfect timing. I greeted Briana and led her into the kitchen.

"You hungry?" I asked.

"You have no idea," she said and stepped forward awkwardly.

I knew she had wanted to hug me but refrained from doing so, which was fine; I felt out of place hugging her, too. I smiled and prepared her a bowl of cheesy noodles.

"Aw, you made KD?" she asked. "That's so sweet."

I shrugged. It wasn't very fancy, but it would suffice. We sat down at the dining room table, both a little shy as usual, and ate our noodles. Maddi and Nathan were still in the living room, huddled on the sofa.

"Whoa," she said.

"What?" I asked, my eyes widening. Was it the food? Was it that bad? Or that good?

"Your face. What the hell happened?" she asked, staring at my right eye.

"Oh," I said, "I fell. Tripped on a purse, actually. Super embarrassing."

"Looks painful. I barely even noticed it though, your hair hides it pretty well," she said.

"Yep, that's the idea," I said and jerked my head sideways to allow most of my hair to fall into my face.

She burst into laughter and shook her head.

"You weirdo," she said.

I lit up and watched her more closely as she shuffled the creamy noodles into her mouth. What would it be like to kiss her sober? I was sure she wanted me to, but I had been pretty clear about wanting someone else. Why was I suddenly thinking like this? Was I falling for her? I couldn't blame her for taking it slow. If anything, it intrigued me. The fact that she wasn't chasing me anymore made me want to chase her, in a strange sense.

"So, tell me about your day," she said.

Tell her about my day? Why hadn't Sam ever asked me this? I shook these thoughts away and focused my energy on the present.

"It was the best. Well, apart from that purse

injury. I don't know, everyone at work is so nice. The concierge, Antonio, is so sweet, and Gloria, one of the receptionists... Hilarious woman." I stopped when I realized I was blabbering, although, she seemed to enjoy my banter. She stared at me, absorbing every word. I shrugged. "I'm happy I'm working again."

"I bet. I don't know how you went on not working for so long. It gets to be depressing, I find," she said.

I suddenly realized that all this time, I had been the topic of every conversation. I didn't know where she worked. Was she in school? I didn't know.

"Hey, I don't know much about you," I said. "Tell me something."

And we went on discussing all sorts of things without alcohol for the first time, meaning I would actually remember. I found out that she worked as a chiropractor's assistant and had just completed college. I learned many other things about her, which only made me more interested. We finished our bowls and I cleaned them in the sink.

"Hey Kaity, we're going out. See you in a bit," Maddi said.

The two lovebirds left, and Briana and I went into the living room. I could barely focus on the TV. All I wanted to do was rest my head on her shoulder. Surely, she felt the same. But I couldn't bring myself to do it. I assumed every movement she made was intentional. When she repositioned herself, I imagined that she was trying to sit closer to me, even if only to brush her thigh against mine. I was probably overanalyzing everything. We finished a stand-up comedy and Briana yawned.

"I better head out," she said. "Gotta get up early for work."

"Yeah, me too. Well, the getting up early part. I don't have to go anywhere. I mean, I live here, so," I said, ranting nervously again.

She shook her head and smiled at me. "You're cute," she said.

I looked away.

"All right, well, goodnight," she said, the awkwardness returning.

"Goodnight," I said. I hesitated.

After a few seconds of uncertainty, she stretched out her arm and hugged me as I would have hugged one of my male friends; the good ol' tap-on-the-back kind of hug. This had been better than nothing but wasn't what I wanted.

Chapter 22

Work went on as it had the first day—rapidly and filled with entertainment. By Thursday, I was already beginning to feel comfortable with the computer system, and I knew that I would be prepared to work on my own that upcoming Monday. Even though I was focused on what I was doing, I couldn't help feel Antonio staring at me from behind his desk. I quickly glanced up at him. He had this sly smile on his face as if he were trying to be seductive. I couldn't tell for sure, but I knew something was up.

I did my best to ignore him, and it helped when people entered the hotel seeking information.

"All right, you can go eat," Charlene said.

"Huh?" I asked.

"It's lunchtime," she said, "go on."

"Go! Run, my child! Before the beast changes her mind!" Gloria said, shooing me away.

I chuckled, grabbed my things, and left.

Antonio smiled at me as I passed his desk, and I feared he would follow me into the lunchroom. I continued along, trying to listen for any cues that may warn me of his approach. There was nothing. I entered the staff room and sat down at the very corner. I pulled out some more leftover macaroni salad that Maddi seemed to enjoy overproducing, and started to eat.

I couldn't help but think of Sam when she had brought me breakfast in bed—how impressed I had been despite how bland the food had tasted, and how her bright eyes looked up at me for approval. Although all I wanted to do was deny the truth, I missed her so much. I tried to focus on Briana instead, which in a strange sense, helped because she was the opposite of Sam. Briana was a sweet girl. She was dark-skinned, shorter than me, mature, and loved to talk. Sam, on the other hand, was a badass (nice to me when she was sober, mind you), pale as a ghost, slightly taller than me, not very mature, and preferred to do rather than say.

I sighed and took a bite of my macaroni.

KNOCK KNOCK.

I shot a quick glance at the door. Antonio.

"Hello, Kaitlyn," he said.

"Hey, Antonio, how's it going?" I asked.

I tried to be nice, even though I was annoyed that he had intentionally followed me on my lunch break. I enjoyed my alone time.

"I am good, how are you?" He approached my table.

Just leave me alone, I thought. I only get thirty minutes to myself at work.

I swallowed my food. "Um, good."

"Wonderful." He sat down.

Get lost!

"You on break?" I asked, realizing how cold I sounded.

"Yes," he said.

I nodded and kept eating. What was I supposed to say?

"Do you have boyfriend, Kaitlyn? I apologize if this is not polite," he said.

Why was everyone so blunt? Why did I attract such direct people? Did no one have manners anymore?

"Um, well," I said. I felt my face go red. "I have a gir—" but I stopped myself. I knew what he was getting at. But was it really necessary to explain to him that I was a lesbian? I assumed that he would either reject the truth or that he would find me repulsive. "I do," I said and looked away.

He slouched like a kid being told they can't have a cookie.

"Yeah..." I said awkwardly.

I didn't want to ask him why he'd asked me. I knew what he was trying to do. A great guy if I were straight, I'm sure. I knew how good-looking he was, but it did nothing for me. My heart didn't flutter when he looked at me. I didn't get nervous. If anything, I was annoyed. Now with Sam, on the other hand, I often thought that I would never again catch my breath when those piercing eyes met mine.

"Cool," he said and it sounded so funny with his accent—cute, even.

I laughed, and he looked up at me.

"What?" he asked.

"You're a cool guy, Antonio," I said.

This caused him to show off the whitest teeth I had ever seen. My comment alone had made his day, and I was content knowing that I had been the one to make it.

"So what is your boyfriend's name?" he asked.

I was a terrible liar. John? Please. I would have probably blurted out John Smith. So I did what I always did best—I bent the truth.

"Brianaaa... His name is Brian," I said.

"Oh, that is a nice name."

"Yep," I said plainly. I finished my lunch and packed my things.

When I went home that night, I couldn't help but appreciate the humor surrounding the day's event, regardless of how uncomfortable my conversation with Antonio had become. So I called Briana and explained to her what happened, and of course, she laughed too. But what I had failed to realize was that in a sense, I had basically referred to Briana as my girlfriend, even though I had altered her gender for storytelling purposes.

"So, if I were a boy, you'd be my girlfriend? Is that it?" she asked jokingly, but I knew she wasn't kidding.

To avoid any more unnecessary awkwardness, I joined in on the halfhearted joke, "Exactly. You know I love the boys. Too bad you're a girl, Brian-AH."

We laughed it off and I eventually said goodnight and hung up. Since she also worked downtown, she agreed to meet me for lunch the next afternoon. I told her to enter the Inn's main lobby, and that we could leave from there.

When Friday finally rolled around and I had spent the first half of my workday training, Briana walked into the lobby as planned. I was happy to see her when she entered. She was sporting a bright yellow jacket, which accentuated her dark features.

"Hey Kaity," she said, walking up to the counter.

"Hey!" I said. "Charlene, is it all right if I go on my lunch?"

"You don't get lunch today," Charlene said, her face demonstrating no sign of humor whatsoever.

I froze in a half-seated position and looked at Briana.

"Wow, you're easy. Get out of here. Go! Eat!" Charlene said and started laughing.

Phew. I wanted to nudge her, but I didn't feel *that* comfortable with her yet. Maybe after the next joke.

"You're funny," I said with a tone of sarcasm.

I grabbed my jacket and led Briana towards the front doors. Right as we were about to exit, I caught Antonio smiling at Briana, and she returned a friendly nod.

"That's him," I said as we exited.

"Really? He's cute," she said.

"What, are you bi?" I asked. I hadn't intended to sound so defensive, but something inside of me had boiled when I had heard her say she thought Antonio *cute*. Was this jealousy?

"Of course not. But I know when a guy is good-looking," she said. "Don't you?"

"Yeah, I guess you're right. He is a good-looking guy," I said.

"What, are you bi?" she sneered back jokingly.

I playfully shoved her a few feet away from

me. We made our way to Subway for a quick lunch, but kept the conversation superficial.

"A few friends and I are going to Taylor's Tower tonight. Join me?" she asked.

I didn't have any plans, so I accepted her offer.

"Cool. I'm pre-drinking with my best friend, Jacob, so you should join us beforehand, too."

"Sure. That sounds good," I said.

"Great," she said, a huge grin on her face.

We grabbed our jackets and threw away the mess we had created. And for the first time, I reached in to hug her goodbye. The hug must have pleased her; her lips pulled up into a shy smile before she said goodbye.

When I returned to work, I quickly made a run to the bathroom, unaware of the situation I was about to face. As I exited the bathroom door, I ran into Antonio, who stated we were apparently "crossing paths by coincidence."

"Who was your friend?" he asked.

"Huh?" I said.

"Your friend who was just here. She is beautiful. Could you introduce me next time?" he asked.

And that's when I knew Briana was more to me than a friend. How I had fallen for her, I didn't know. But I did know that I was jealous. I felt my face heat up and I shook my head.

"Sorry Antonio. But when I said I had a

boyfriend named Brian, the truth is, I have a girlfriend, and her name is Briana. The girl you saw, well, that's Briana."

I couldn't believe that I was being so direct. It wasn't in my nature. And I knew that Briana wasn't my girlfriend, but I didn't know how else to explain it. A half-lie was my best approach.

"I'm sorry," he said, forcing a smile. "I do not understand."

He frowned as if trying to put puzzle pieces together.

"Well, it's like I said: I don't have a boyfriend. I have a girlfriend. She's my lover, my partner. Do you know what I mean?" I said.

His smile slowly twisted itself into pure disgust.

"You are sleeping with a woman?" he asked.

"Well, I'm not sleeping with her. But I'm a lesbian, if that's what you're getting at," I said.

I wondered if this had been a mistake, but I didn't much care at this point. He was of no importance to me, and I didn't need anyone creating unnecessary stress in my life right now.

"That is against God—do you know that?" he asked.

My heart skipped a beat. Here we go. Did I want to knock him one in the face? Yes. But at the same time, he was entitled to his belief.

"I'm sorry you feel that way, Antonio. I'm

not a bad person, but I was born this way, okay?" I said. There was nothing else to be said.

"No, you are sinful. You are a bad person. God will punish you. Do not talk to me anymore," and with that, he walked away.

I stood still for a moment, trying hard to absorb what had happened. My throat swelling, I rushed back into the bathroom to release my emotions into a bunch of toilet paper.

How could anyone say such horrible things to another human being? It didn't make any sense to me. Why would God punish his own creation? It wasn't as though I had decided to be gay—no one simply *decides* to be something that will inevitably cause a great deal of hardship throughout one's lifetime. How could people be so ignorant? Even some animals have been proven to be gay, for crying out loud. Clearly, it isn't a conscious decision.

I took a deep breath, gathered my emotions, and went back to the reception counter. I hoped Charlene and Gloria wouldn't notice my red, swollen eyes. Fortunately, they did not. I spent the remainder of my day boiling inside, refusing to look at Antonio. When I went home that night, Maddi wasn't there to listen to me vent. I found a little note posted to the fridge which read, "Gone out with Nathan, see you tomorrow. Mashed potatoes in the fridge."

So I aggressively tore the fridge door open

and peered inside. I didn't want to call Briana. I didn't want to be that annoying girl who complains about her problems. So I grabbed a cold beer from the fridge and skipped supper.

Surely the night would make up for the day's crappiness. After a few beers, my nerves relaxed, and my muscles loosened. I threw on some fresh clothes and dialed Briana's number for directions. Fortunately, her friend Jacob didn't live far at all—one bus ride away. So I went out into the cold, winter streets and caught my bus. When I arrived at my destination, Briana's greeting seemed to make everything better.

"Hey stranger," she said, resting her face against the open door, "come on in."

The apartment wasn't very big, but it was well decorated. There were beautiful paintings all over the walls and healthy green plants positioned on slim glass tables.

"Hey there," said a cute, unusually thin, brown-haired boy. His features were so delicate, so smooth, and there wasn't a doubt in my mind he was gay.

"Come here," he said and wrapped his bony arms around me. I hugged him back awkwardly. "You must be Kaity," he said.

I looked over at Briana, who grinned and sat down.

"Yeah. And you, Jacob?" I asked. How I

remembered the name Briana had mentioned, I had no idea. But woohoo—brownie points for me!

"Yep, that's me," he said. "So, I guess you ladies are taking me out to meet some women," he said and sipped on his sky-blue drink. "I'm so excited."

I wasn't sure whether or not he was being sarcastic, but I liked him. I could tell he had a good sense of humor, even though I had yet to understand it. We ended up playing Twister—which I always thought was the funniest game to play when drinking.

The rest of the night turned out as it always did; bright lights, loud music, mindless chatter, and drunkenness. Nearing the end of our outing, I had enough drinks in me to do about anything. And even though I should have blacked out at that point, I remember Briana taking my hand at the back of the club and moving in for a gentle kiss. I didn't back away. I stared at her, my heavy, drunken eyes filled with content.

When I woke up the next morning, my hangover routine hadn't changed. I lay there, wondering if Briana would have kissed me had we been sober. Probably not. I didn't blame her, either. I wouldn't have wanted to kiss a girl knowing that she was constantly thinking about someone else.

The rest of my weekend went by smoothly. It was back to work on Monday, and the days went on. Antonio no longer spoke to me, Gloria and Charlene made me smile at least ten times per day, Briana and I grew closer, and Maddi was now officially seeing Nathan. Some weekends, Briana and I stayed in, while others, we went out and got drunk. We both avoided labeling our relationship, as she knew I didn't want to complicate anything, which really, was selfish on my part. I had to let go of Sam.

To further show her that I was committed to trying, I did what I thought I'd never have the balls to do. I kissed her, sober. It was a Thursday night when the two of us were alone at her place. We were sitting on her white loveseat (which I thought was pretty romantic), and I just did it. How? I don't know. I leaned in and kissed her. And although her taste wasn't quite as delicious as Sam's, I knew I'd be able to find it in me to care about this girl.

Months went by, and things only improved. Antonio quit his position as concierge to continue his hospitality dreams at a competitor's nearby hotel. Hey, fine by me. I talked to Briana about going back to school. Although I had once wanted to be a Science teacher, I now wanted to be a nurse. It would take several years of studying, but I was willing to put in the work.

I was so overwhelmed by new emotions and by new dreams, that I failed to remember the one thing that had ever mattered to me before: Sam. I was too distracted with my life to even ponder her existence. Was she even alive? I tried not to think about it. What good would it do? I began browsing the Internet at work, analyzing every detail of my education plan. Charlene was all for it.

Gloria, on the other hand, had specifically said, "Sweetheart, if you want to pick up shit for the rest of your life, go walk dogs."

I knew she hadn't meant it. Perhaps she'd had a terrible experience with a nurse in the past; or, perhaps a loved one was a nurse who unloaded the daily burdens of work on her. Who knew? Either way, I wasn't about to change my mind.

And right when the pieces started to fit into the most exquisite puzzle I could have imagined for myself, a gust of wind entered the lobby, shattering it to bits. I looked up when I heard the hotel's front doorbells clatter, followed by wet, squeaky footsteps.

There she was.

Her shoulder-length black hair was drenched, as were her clothes. Her mascara was still intact, and her glowing, green eyes pierced me. I thought my heart would stop, or at the very least, that my lungs would cave due to lack of oxygen.

She tilted her head, released a tired breath, and said, "I lost my umbrella."

Chapter 23

I couldn't move or speak. I simply sat there staring. Charlene didn't detect the change in the atmosphere. She pulled out a pen and smiled at Sam.

"Hi there. Sorry to hear you lost your umbrella. Do you have a reservation?" she asked.

"Sort of," Sam said, her eyes narrowing on me.

This was it. I was going to die. She had either returned to kill me, or... Well, that was the only plausible explanation I could think of. Charlene followed Sam's eyes, only to find my pale, frightened face. Everything went quiet, and I hadn't the slightest idea what to do.

"Kaity, can I talk to you for a sec?" Sam asked, smiling at me.

My heart sank at the sound of my name. No, please no. Surely, that smile wasn't sincere.

She'd lost her mind. I was dead. I wanted to run. I wanted to drop underneath the counter and pretend I didn't exist. Why was she here? And why was I being so paranoid? It felt as if I had done something wrong. I suddenly thought about Briana, and a heavy weight fell onto my shoulders. I had cheated on Sam. No! I hadn't. I wasn't with Sam. I hadn't seen Sam in months!

"Please," she pleaded.

Her voice was much softer this time, and I knew that something was up. She wasn't there to hurt me. She was hurt. The realization penetrated my paranoid thinking, and I jumped to my feet and nodded.

"O—Of course," I said, walking around the reception desk. "You okay?"

"Yeah," she mumbled and looked up at Charlene.

I followed her eyes and smiled at Charlene.

"Hey, is it all right if I take a quick break?" I asked.

"No worries, kid. Come back when you're ready," Charlene said.

"Here, this way," I said, and led her into the staff room.

She was drenched. Where had she come from? As I grabbed a bunch of napkins to wipe her down, I could sense she was staring at me. My throat swelled. I had missed her so much.

I looked up and met her bright eyes.

"Hey," she said.

"Hey," I said. I looked away and smiled shyly.

Fortunately for me, the seats in the staff room were made of leather, so I didn't have to worry about her dampening the chairs. I asked her to sit, and I kneeled in front of her and began wiping her clothes and skin. I could sense her eyes still on me; I did my best to ignore her, which was difficult. I bit down hard on my lower lip to avoid showing any unnecessary emotion, but it was useless. My bottom lip trembled and my throat swelled until it ached.

I hadn't the strength.

She suddenly wrapped her cold hand around the back of my neck and pulled me in, tight against her chest. I gave in. It was all I wanted to do. I inhaled her perfume, squeezed fistfuls of her leather jacket, and allowed my head to rest against her body as I listened to her heart race.

Regardless of how chilled and damp her jacket was, this was the warmest sensation I'd felt in a very long time. I wanted to stay there forever. I wanted to fall asleep in her arms and never again regain consciousness. She placed her other hand against my head and squeezed me hard.

"I'm so sorry," she whispered.

I didn't reply. I couldn't. Tears slid down my

cheeks. I rewrapped my arms around her and held her close. When her embrace finally loosened, I backed away and looked at her face—the angelically white, sharp-featured face that I had fallen in love with. I noticed black makeup smudged underneath her eyes that wasn't caused by the rain. I could see now that her red, bloodshot eyes reflected pain, as they searched for something inside of me.

"Please," she said and sniffled up the excess moisture dripping from her nose. She looked down and swallowed hard. "I love you. I've changed, I swear. Please come back. I'm clean. I promise. I need you, Kaity. I—" and tears came pouring out.

The sight was excruciating. No matter the amount of suffering she'd caused me, never once would I have wished it be returned to her. I grabbed her face and allowed my lips to gently touch hers. Her warm tears slid around the edges of my thumbs, and she exhaled the most satisfied breath. She pulled me in tight again and kissed me harder before kissing my cheeks and my neck.

"I've missed you so much," she said.

"I've missed you too," was all I could say, even though my emotions were far greater than a few measly words.

I couldn't express to her what I'd gone through. I don't believe words could ever truly describe my heartache. Instead, I imagined that everything would fall into place—that Sam and I would be together again for years to come... for the remainder of our lives.

But the reality of it all collided with my wishful thinking. What now? Yes, we had missed each other. But what about Briana? What about my life? Would she screw me over again? Was I supposed to move back in with her? Was she lying about being clean? She was a good liar, that much I knew. Although I didn't want to think about the negative, these thoughts were impossible to avoid. And I knew that she knew it, too. She looked up at me and smiled.

"Here," she said, handing me a crumpled piece of paper. "I don't want to mess anything up for you... But I swear, I'm different now. I have a job. I moved out. I wouldn't have changed if it weren't for you. I'm in love with you," she looked away. "Please call me... We can talk some more later, over coffee maybe, rather than beer."

This calmed me. Perhaps she was telling the truth. I gently grabbed the piece of paper from her soft fingertips and nodded. She kissed my forehead and backed me away so she could stand. I didn't want her to leave. I wanted to solve all of this right now. But I knew it was impossible. I had to return to work, and she probably had her own things to do.

"I love you," she said, before exiting the staff room.

I stayed there on my knees, my face soaked with a mixture of tears and rainwater. I felt so pathetic, there on the floor. I looked down at the little piece of paper and closed my eyes. This wasn't going to be easy.

Chapter 24

"Hey you," came Briana's voice. I nearly jumped out of my skin when I noticed her leaning against the hotel's exterior wall. "Need a ride?" she asked, dangling her set of car keys.

"H—Hey," I stammered. I could barely look at her.

What had I done? I knew what I had done. I had kissed Sam, knowing all too well that I would take her back. What was I supposed to do about Briana? I cared about her. Sickening nausea crept into my stomach. I felt like a cheater.

Why had Sam come back? I was finally gaining control of my life. I attempted a weak smile at Briana, but the guilt was unbearable. I followed her to her car and hopped in.

"Why are you so quiet?" she asked, glancing my way.

"Ah, long day, that's all," I said and forced

yet another smile.

What the hell was I going to do? It felt as though Sam's number was burning a hole in my pocket. I knew that the piece of paper was there, and I knew that I would call.

"Hey, so I rented the greatest movie ever. I can't tell you what it is yet. It's a surprise," Briana said, visibly excited.

This was unbearable.

"Kaity?" she asked.

"Hmm?" I said.

"What's wrong?"

I wanted to tell her everything, but I wasn't ready. I had to lie, as much as it hurt me to do so.

"I... I don't know. I feel sick. Would you mind if I stayed in tonight?" I asked.

"Aw, well," she hesitated, "how about you let me take care of you? I'll make you some soup, and we can watch that movie. I don't wanna go out either," she said.

Why did she have to be so wonderful? So kind to me?

"That's so sweet, Briana. But, I don't know. I think I need to be alone tonight. I'm sorry. Please don't be mad."

"Oh," was all she said.

We had not spent a weekend apart in several months now, so I didn't blame her for being upset. Had I been in her shoes, I'd have likely felt suspicious, too—hurt, even.

The remainder of the ride home was quiet. Right when she pulled into Maddi's driveway, I grabbed my bag and thanked her for the ride. I couldn't kiss or hug her. I felt awful.

"Hey, Kaity," Briana called out, right before I closed the car door.

"Yeah?" I asked, leaning into the car.

"Did I do something wrong?" she asked.

My throat swelled.

"No, not at all," I reassured her. "I feel really sick and weird. I'll call you in a bit though, okay?" I said and closed the door.

I watched as she pulled out of the driveway and drove off. I wondered what she was thinking and if I had truly upset her. I sighed and walked into the house. Fortunately, Maddi was home. When I entered, she was cuddled up in the living room, reading a sci-fi novel.

"Hey, long time no see," she said, smirking at me.

"Hey," I said.

"What's wrong? Kaity, I know something's wrong. What happened?" she asked, suddenly jolting upright.

I dropped my bag and bowed my head as if this would somehow mask my pain.

"Kaity?" Maddi pressed. She rushed over to me. "What's wrong? Did that bitch break up with you?!"

I smiled up at her, content with how protective she was of me.

"No," I said.

"Then what is it?" she asked.

I rubbed my forehead and sighed heavily.

"Sam," I said.

"What?" she asked. Her eyes opened wide and she stared at me.

"She came in today," I said.

"And...?" Maddi asked.

"She's changed. She wants me back," I said. Maddi snorted.

"Well you aren't going back, right? I mean, she's been nothing but trouble."

I looked up at her, my slanted eyebrows expressing precisely what she feared.

"Kaity? You aren't. Right?" she said slowly. "You aren't going back. Please tell me you aren't going back."

"I'm still in love with her. What do you want me to say?" I said, and I bit my lip.

"Oh sweetheart," Maddi said and pulled me into her arms before tears streamed down my cheeks. I wiped my eyes and rested my chin on her shoulder. "I know you care about her," she said, "but you're doing so good with your life now. You have to let her go."

"I know," I blubbered.

"Oh, honey. Go get some rest. Think it over. You'll realize how irrational this is, okay?" she said, cupping her palms around my face.

I nodded and walked away. Think it over—that was the last thing I wanted to do. I knew precisely how irrational my desires were, but I couldn't help myself. Surely, Sam wasn't lying. Maybe she'd changed, and everything would be better now.

I dropped into bed and went to sleep. That was all I could do now. Besides, I was too tired to do anything else. When I woke up at eleven p.m., I realized I had slept quite a bit longer than planned. I reached for my phone to view my messages: there were three new ones.

1: Briana—6:46 p.m.: "Hey, what r u doing?"

2: Briana—7:57 p.m.: "Are u all right?"

3: Briana—10:31 p.m.: "Kaity, if ur mad at me, say so. Stop ignoring me."

I quickly hit respond to let her know that I had fallen asleep and that I wasn't angry. I wasn't being fair to her. What was I going to do? I wished I would have never woken up. But as I stared at my phone, I knew precisely what I was about to do. I created a new message:

"You awake?"

I dialed the number Sam had given me and hit send. A mistake? Maybe. But it felt right, and I knew that if I didn't do it then, I would do it the next day, or the next week, or even the next month. Within minutes, I received a response.

"Yes I am. Can I see u?"

My heart sank. I wanted to see her more than anything. Was she drunk, though? It was Friday night; surely she had been partying. But no matter how irresponsible I knew I was being, I asked for her new address and called a cab. Fortunately, Maddi was sleeping.

When I arrived at the apartment, it wasn't at all what I expected. The building was extremely run down, and its location wasn't one I would have picked out myself. I shot glances from side to side as I entered the front doors, afraid of who may be lurking around a nearby corner, waiting to pounce on me for money. I scanned the ringer buttons: Bowa.

Geez. This place was too cheap to afford a few more letters. Surely this was her apartment. I beeped her.

"Hey. Come up," she said, her voice electronically modified.

I soon found myself standing in front of door 402. This was it. At once, an irrational thought crossed my mind. Had she lured me here to kill me? Of course, this thought was absurd, but I was never entirely certain with Sam. She was always so unpredictable. Before I could contemplate this silly, morbid idea any further, the front door opened.

"Hey," she said, grinning at me.

She was clad in a clean white T-shirt with black sweatpants. This was her comfortable look. I was impressed. Comfort on a Friday night. I wondered if there was anyone else in the apartment, but she cut me short when she noticed me stretching my neck to see inside.

"Relax. I'm alone."

I followed her inside and removed my boots.

"Nice place," I said.

It was a blatant lie. The place was a mess. The kitchen counters were piled with dirty dishes, the sofas had clearly been purchased at a flea market, and the tiny fifteen-inch tube TV was sure to strain any viewer's eyes.

"I know it's a shit hole, Kaity," she said. "You can be honest with me."

"Okay. This place is a shit hole," I admitted. "How did you end up here?"

She didn't answer. Instead, she gently grabbed my hand and led me to the sofa.

"Sit with me."

"Seriously... Why'd you move here?" I persisted.

"I had no other choice," she sighed. "I blew all of my money on... Well, you know."

I blinked. I couldn't believe it. Had her addiction gone that far?

"Are you serious? How is that even possible? You had thousands!"

"Yeah, I'm aware of that Kaity," she said sharply. "I was dumb, okay?"

She looked away.

I laid a hand on her lap. "I'm sorry, Sam. I wasn't trying to offend you. I'm shocked."

"Well, it doesn't matter anymore. I'm done. I haven't touched a drop or a pill in two months, and I'm never getting back into that mess. I swear, Kaity, I've changed." And her weak, helpless eyes proved to me that she wasn't lying.

"Well, in that case, I'm really happy for you," I said earnestly.

"I don't care if you're happy for me; I want you to be happy with me," she said, staring at me. "Look, I stopped because I need you. I know it took a while for me to see it, but now I do."

I can't quite explain how I felt. I was ecstatic that the love of my life wanted me as much as I wanted her. But at the same time, I was terrified. I knew all too well the power she had over me. With Sam, I was either on top of the world, or I was down on the ground, scraping at mud to feed myself. There was no gray area with her, and this, I believe, attracted the same results; I was either going to stay with her, or I would have to abandon her and never look back.

"Please," she begged.

She grabbed my shirt and pulled me on top of her. I didn't resist. We lay together for a while, listening to each other breathe.

"Sam, I'm seeing someone," I said, my face smothered in her neck.

She pulled me back and held my face, her green eyes glued to me. For a moment, I thought she might hit me. But I then realized that her energy was loving, not hateful.

"I don't care," she said. "You could have twenty girlfriends, but in the end, you know we're meant for each other."

I smiled at her.

"Don't get cocky."

She snorted and huddled closer again.

"Kaity, I love you. If you don't love me, that's fine. But I love you."

"You're a dork," I said.

I felt her giggle underneath me.

"You know how I feel about you; stop using it to your advantage," I said.

"You know I use everything to my advantage," she said and squeezed me hard.

We stayed up discussing everything and anything until the sun joined us in the morning. Apparently, Sam had started working at a nearby warehouse in the shipping and receiving section. She said the work would have to do until she was back on her feet. She had also cut all contact with her friends being that they were nothing but bad influences.

I told her about work, Maddi, and Briana. I noticed her nostrils flare every time I mentioned Briana's name, and I do admit that I loved her reaction. And although we had not touched a drop of alcohol that night, I felt drunk by the time morning came around. The orange, morning sunlight came blasting through the window, creating a triangular design on the carpet beside us. She fell asleep in my arms, her body pressed up against mine. With the tips of my fingers, I brushed her dark hair out of her face and watched her sleep for a while. She was so perfect. I closed my eyes and allowed myself to be overwhelmed by these new emotions, before I too fell asleep.

* * *

I was shaken out of sleep by the persistent high-pitched sound being projected from my cell phone. Sam moaned but didn't wake when I rolled her away from my body and crawled down from the sofa. I rushed to find my jacket and removed my phone from its inner pocket. It was Briana calling. I felt a sudden surge of panic in my chest. I couldn't answer.

What would I say? What if she wanted to see me? Worse yet, what if she knew I wasn't home? I squinted back at the VCR (yes, that's right, an old-school VCR—she should have had Blu-ray by now) to see what time it was: 3:46 p.m. Shit! I was now certain Briana knew I hadn't slept at home. Surely, she had called Maddi, worried that I had perhaps passed out due to my *illness*. When the ringing finally stopped, I opened my phone only to see that she had attempted to call me seven times earlier. I was done for.

I held my breath and stared at the wall. I wasn't a cheater. We weren't even technically together, I reminded myself. But I would have to tell her about Sam. Deep down, I already knew that I wasn't about to let go of the one person I wanted most of all. So I did what any other liar would do and called Maddi to find out whether or not Briana had called. I was disgusted with myself.

"Where the hell are you?" was the first thing Maddi said.

Uh oh.

"Hey, sorry, I..." I hesitated. "I went to my parents' place and fell asleep there. I forgot to charge my phone."

Wow. I was a great liar when I wanted to be. It made me feel awful.

"Oh," she said, "well, are you okay? Briana's been calling like crazy, thinking you're dead or something."

Poor Briana. She was worried sick about me, while I had been holding the one person I loved more than anything in the world all through the night.

"I'm okay. I'll call Briana now and let her know. Sorry about that," I said.

"Ugh." She hung up. Clearly, she didn't like being the middleman—well, woman.

"What's wrong?" Sam moaned, her tired eyes barely open.

I smiled up at her as if the mere sound of her voice had obliterated all of my problems.

"Nothing, it's fine," I said.

"Mmm..."

I crawled back onto the sofa and snuggled up beside her. I kissed her cheek and her tender, pink lips.

"Good morning," she said, her bright eyes searching me.

"Morning? Good afternoon, miss," I said and kissed her again.

But all of this joy and warmth seemed to evaporate when I realized that I was in fact, cheating on my label-less girlfriend.

"I have to tell her," I said.

"Tell who?" Sam asked, still groggy.

"Briana."

Sam growled.

"Shut up. I mean it. This is cheating. I'm not that person," I said.

"You're right. Then call her," Sam said.

"And what? Break up over the telephone? That's a little immature, don't you think?" I said.

"All right, then go see her, have the awkward conversation, turn red, then ask her to drive you back home." She laughed.

"This isn't funny," I said.

Her smile faded. "Look, I know it isn't easy, but you have to make a decision."

I rolled my eyes. "Don't act all innocent. You know what my decision is."

She pulled me in and chuckled.

"Well, then, you have to communicate your decision to the person you're going to release," she said, her tone suggestive.

"Release," I repeated. "Way to make me out to be the captivator."

"You are the captivator. You've captivated my heart," she sang.

"Ew. Corny. Shut up." I slapped her on the shoulder.

She burst out laughing, but her features quickly hardened.

"All right, in all seriousness though. Call her, see her, I don't care. But you have to tell her. I don't share."

I sighed and rested my head on her warm, cushion chest. She was right. I had to tell Briana immediately. But how? I didn't want to see her in person; I knew precisely what was going to happen. I was either going to get punched in the face or be witness to her tears. Both of these possibilities, in my opinion, were equally painful.

I grabbed my phone and went into Sam's bedroom to be alone. I dialed Briana's number and held my breath, as I promised myself to sugarcoat everything.

"Hello?" she said, sounding incredibly disconcerted.

"Hey," I said.

"Kaity, what's wrong? Are you okay? You've been ignoring me all night, and all of today," she said.

"I'm so sorry, really," I said.

"What is it?" she asked.

I fell silent.

"Kaity?"

"Yeah?"

"What is it?" she repeated.

I inhaled... and exhaled.

"Briana, remember when we first met?" I asked.

"Yeah..." she said slowly.

"And I told you I was still, well, not over a certain someone?" I said.

"Sam. Yeah. I remember," she said coldly, then paused.

"Well, she came to see me at work yesterday."

Briana went silent, and I squeezed my eyes shut. This was so difficult.

"I... I don't know, it made me think about all sorts of things, and I think I should be alone for a while," I said.

"So you're going back to your ex?" she said

bluntly. And there it was—the anger. She had every right.

"No, that's not what I said. All I said was it threw me off, and it made me realize what relationships do to people," I said. I couldn't be forthcoming about everything. It would hurt her too much. "I think I'm better off alone right now." I closed my eyes and hoped that this would suffice.

"Great," she said and hung up.

I turned over and hugged Sam's pillow. What had I done? I clenched my jaw and remained still as warm tears slid down my face only to be absorbed by the soft cotton of Sam's pillowcase.

"You okay?" Sam asked as she slowly entered the room.

Shrugging, I wiped my cheeks.

She climbed into bed with me. "Bad, huh?"

"Yeah."

"Hey." She wrapped her arm around me. "I know it's hard giving up something that means a lot to you, but I won't let you down. We should have never separated in the first place."

I nodded and wrapped my fingers around hers, with nothing left to do but hope that everything would turn out the way I had once envisioned.

Chapter 25

"I'll be back in a bit. Wish me luck!" I said and closed the door behind me.

This was it. It was time to tell Maddi. In all honesty, the nausea in my stomach was far greater than it had been before telling Briana the truth. Why? Because Maddi had been there with me through everything. She knew the heartache Sam's addiction had caused me. She'd seen it all. Would she take this news lightly? Unlikely.

Sam had asked me to move in with her again, and although deep down I knew that this was a gamble, I couldn't bring myself to refuse. I was giving up everything; a wonderful home with Maddi, a relationship with Briana, and my stable frame of mind. All for what? To be with Sam. Was it worth it? Only time would tell. And no matter how hard I tried to talk myself out of it, the results were always the same. My selfish feelings for Sam overpowered all other aspects of my life.

"Wow, you're finally home," Maddi said as I entered the front door.

"Yeah," I mumbled.

"You weren't at your parents'." She glared at me.

I looked up at her, my eyebrows leveled unevenly.

"Where were you?" she asked. Her eyes showed absolutely no sign of amusement.

I laughed nervously and shook my head.

"Why would you say I wasn't at my parents'?" I asked.

"Because I called them. I knew you were lying, so I wanted to confirm."

I felt violated. Okay, so she knew I had lied. But to call my parents? Who did she think she was, my girlfriend? She had no right to ask where I had spent the night.

"Why do you care where I was?" I asked.

"Because I was the one stuck dealing with Briana's phone calls!" she snapped. I noticed her nostrils flare, and I didn't speak. "And you're supposed to be my best friend! Why the hell would you lie to me about such a ridiculous thing?" she asked.

"I don't know, okay?" I said, the volume of my voice increasing along with hers. "I broke it off with Briana."

Her jaw dropped, and she pointed an accusing finger at me.

"You were with Sam, weren't you?"

"What does it matter?" I asked.

"It matters! Were you, or weren't you?" I had never seen her this angry before. I'd hoped this wouldn't happen, but there was no way out now. I wasn't going to lie to her a second time, and I wasn't going to sugarcoat anything; we were clearly beyond that.

"Yeah, I was," I said bluntly.

"And are you going back?" she asked, her words slowing as if to ensure my absolute understanding.

"Yeah," I said.

She threw her head back and grabbed her hair.

"Ugh. Damn it, Kaity. I love you, but you can be such an idiot sometimes. Listen, I'm sorry," she said, now pacing back and forth, "but you have to go. Pack your things, I can't do this again."

"Do what?" I asked.

"Do what? Are you kidding me? I can't be the only guest invited to another one of your three-month pity parties when Sam decides to leave you again!"

I wasn't sure which hurt more—the fact that she had just insinuated Sam and I weren't going to last, or the fact that she'd referred to my depression as a pathetic pity party. I simply nodded and walked away. I had a lot to pack.

When I was done, I grabbed my bags and headed for the front door.

"I can give you a ride," Maddi offered, her tone ridden with guilt.

"I'd rather walk," I said coldly. I turned around and left.

"Kaity!" Maddi called out.

I stopped halfway in the driveway and looked back at her.

"What?" I said.

"Look, I know you're mad right now. But if you need me, call me, okay?" she said.

I ignored her and walked away. I wouldn't need her, and I most definitely wouldn't call her. I shuffled around the corner of the block, struggling with my bags. When I could no longer see Maddi's house, I dropped my belongings onto the grass and called a cab. Pffft, I wasn't actually going to walk. I had only wanted her to *think* that I was walking to worsen the guilt she felt. Juvenile, I know.

I handed the cab driver a twenty when I arrived at Sam's and hopped out, my bags nearly unmanageable. He offered to help, but I refused and told him to keep the change. Now all I had to do was hope to reach Sam's apartment without getting mugged. Fortunately, I made it, and Sam was sleeping on the sofa when I arrived.

"Don't you lock your door?" I asked, throwing my stuff on the floor with a bang.

Sam suddenly kicked her legs out into the air and swung her arms around so frantically that I couldn't help but laugh. Her eyes were so round and fearful.

"Shit! You scared the hell out of me!"

I cracked up and shook my head.

"See. I could have been a robber," I said.

But apparently, she didn't find this funny. She moaned and rolled over to hide her face in the sofa's cushions. I brought my things into her room, but sat down on her bed rather than continuing to unpack. I observed every detail of her bedroom: the old brown dresser, the stained carpet, the tiny closet, and of course, the broken light bulb resting innocently on her floor.

Poor Sam, but also, poor me. I had given up a wonderful house with Maddi to live here, but it was incomparable. I loved Sam. Sure, I was giving up a lot. Yet in the end, the trade-off was worth it.

Things slowly picked up as the weeks went by. I can't even begin to describe the joy I felt being with Sam. I may not have had much materially, but emotionally, I felt content. I had spoken to neither Maddi nor Briana since our last conversations. And to be honest, I had no intention of contacting either one of them, especially not Briana. I still felt guilty for having abandoned her so unexpectedly to fulfill my own selfish desires.

By the time summer came rolling around, we had finally replaced Sam's entertainment unit with a brand new big-screen Samsung TV and a PS3 to watch Blu-rays. Sam hadn't touched a drink, and she constantly reassured me that she had no temptation whatsoever. Her new addiction was hot chocolate. Hey, that was fine by me.

Everything seemed to fall into place day by day, and I couldn't believe my eyes when Sam came in one evening, dancing and singing absolute nonsense. At first, I assumed she was drunk.

"What the hell are you doing?" I asked, not sure whether or not to laugh.

"I got a promotion! I got a promotion!" she sang, shaking her behind.

I laughed and pulled her into my arms. If there was one feeling in the world more enjoyable than eating chocolate or having sex, it was the joy I felt when I saw Sam's animated features.

"To what? What are you doing now? How'd it happen?" I asked.

I could barely get my words across to her as she sang and danced in my arms. Looking back to when I first met her, I can confirm with absolute certainty that Sam had never been so happy while drinking as she had been during those last few months she spent sober with me.

"I'm the manager," she said proudly, finally regaining composure.

"Shut up," I said, unable to absorb what she had told me.

"Seriously. No lie. My bitch of a manager got fired, and I was selected to take her place."

"No way!" I pulled her in again and kissed her head. "Aw, Sam, that's awesome!"

"I know," she said and squeezed me hard.

I hugged her back and we stood there, enveloped in each other's warmth.

"Hey," she said, pulling back.

"Yeah?"

The excitement had somehow faded. I noticed joy in her eyes, but it wasn't the type led on by exterior events.

"Thanks for believing in me," she said.

I couldn't respond. I simply smiled at her, held her face, and kissed her.

"You just wait," she said, her mood suddenly altering again. "I'm gonna buy us a house, a pool, and so many TVs you'll get sick of television!" she said.

I was so proud of her. I grabbed her arm and forced her into the bedroom. She didn't resist, but rather, enjoyed my aggression. I was so overwhelmed by emotion that I wanted to make her feel what I felt. I raised her shirt and caressed her soft belly. Little goosebumps appeared around her belly button, and I made my way up to her chest. She grabbed my head and exhaled an excited breath. I loved every sound she made, and I wasn't going to stop so long as she continued to breathe the way she did. I pushed her down on the bed. She submitted easily.

"You're so passionate," she breathed.

I was so focused, I couldn't respond. I teased her with the tip of my tongue and gradually made my way down between her inner thighs. My warm breath mixed with the heat of her body, and she wrapped her fingers in my hair. Slowly, I removed her panties and smirked up at her, before making her body feel physically what I was feeling emotionally.

Chapter 26

I heard the front door slam shut, and I glanced up from behind my cheesy romance novel. Something was wrong, and I could have concluded this even before meeting Sam's impatient eyes.

"What's wrong?" I asked.

"Nothing," she said coldly and disappeared into the bedroom.

I stared at the wall for a moment, contemplating whether or not this was the wisest time to approach her, but knowing very well that if I didn't confront the issue now, I wouldn't be able to focus on my novel. I got up and followed her into the bedroom. She sat at the edge of her bed, slouching.

"Sam?" I said.

Nothing. She stared at the floor as if nothing else in the world existed beyond her thoughts. Slowly, I moved in and sat beside her without a word. I would wait for her to come to me. The one-minute wait seemed to last an hour, but she finally sighed.

"I saw my mom," she said.

My eyes bulged out. "What?"

"My mom. Today. I saw her downtown. She recognized me," she said.

I didn't know how to respond, so I kept tight-lipped.

"She's a walking skeleton. She told me to go get some milk for the house, otherwise, my dad would be upset. My dad doesn't even live in Loshano, and I have no clue what she's doing here."

"Oh Sam, I'm so sorry. What did you say?"

"Nothing. I told her the milk would be there when she came home," she said.

I rested my chin on her shoulder and grabbed her clammy hand. I was utterly lost for words. Nothing I could say would change Sam's current state of mind. I couldn't begin to imagine what she was going through. Her mother was a stranger to her—a helpless woman, even.

"I can't help her," Sam said. "You should have seen her, Kaity. I'm surprised she isn't dead yet."

I parted my lips to speak, but Sam stood up. "Listen, I'm going to get some fresh air, I'll be back in a bit."

I simply nodded, and Sam was out the door. All I could do now was hope that she would be all right. I switched on the TV, lay on the sofa, and dozed off to the hypnotizing combination of sounds and luminescent flashes.

The sound of the front door blasting open shook me to full consciousness. I looked back, feeling as though my stomach would climb out of me. She was drunk. There was no doubt about that. She stumbled in, but then lost her balance and fell forward. Her forehead cracked loudly against the wall. She was now shuffling around on her hands and knees. She mumbled a few words, but I couldn't understand what she was saying. Surely, her words were entirely meaningless anyway.

Closing my eyes, I wished the sight away, but it was hopeless. I didn't bother trying to speak to her. She would either yell at me or hit me. Unfortunately, my attempt at remaining invisible didn't last long.

"The... The fuck are you... I'm not stupid," she said, pointing an accusing finger at me.

"What?" I asked.

"Yeah, whatever. D—Don't even, Kaity... Don't even," she slurred.

She disappeared into the bedroom and slammed the door shut. I didn't follow her. I remained awake for nearly the rest of the night, staring into absolute nothingness and debating with myself as to whether or not I had made the gravest mistake of my life by moving back in.

I dropped in and out of consciousness throughout the morning, and when it was time to get up, I could barely open my eyes. I forced myself into a seated position and stretched my stiff limbs. I had to go to work, regardless of the current situation. I was certain that Sam wouldn't be going in to work. Very responsible of a manager, I know.

The day went by horribly. All I could think about was returning to Sam to either yell at her or threaten to leave. I was infuriated. She had been doing so well. Why throw it away now? Over what? Over the past? Sure, she was upset, and I understood that. But she had to be strong. Why hadn't she talked to me, rather than go out to get wasted? I think what pissed me off the most was that she lied about it. Had she told me, "Listen, I need a drink. I haven't felt this stressed in a long time," then I would have understood. But to blatantly lie and tell me that she was going to catch some fresh air?

My heart raced as I walked into the apartment building. What would I even say to her? What if she wasn't home? I unlocked the apartment door and entered. Sam was there, spread out on the sofa, watching TV.

"Hey," she said.

"Hi," I said coldly.

"Kaity, come here, please," she said. Her words were so gentle. She knew I was angry.

I dropped my bag and approached the sofa.

"What?" I asked.

She reached for my hand and sat upright.

"Look, I messed up, okay? I'm so sorry... You can't expect me to be perfect. I'm not getting myself into drugs. You know that."

"Yeah, well, that's how it starts. First, it's the beer, then you'll be popping whatever it was you were taking, and then..." I ranted.

"Stop it," she said, smiling at me. She cupped my face with her warm palms and kissed my lips. How did she do it? How had I gone from being so incredibly angry to feeling so calm, so loved? "I'm not going back, I promise," she said.

I wanted to believe her. She must have sensed the doubt in my eyes; she kissed me again, pulling away slowly.

"I promise," she repeated.

I nodded. All right, so one slipup. It was bound to happen. There was no use arguing about it now. It was the past. All we had to work with was our future, and if Sam was promising to stay clean, then surely, she was going to stay clean.

And if only I had known how painfully wrong I had been that very day, I would have attempted to better prepare myself for what was to come. She did remain true to her promise for another month, that is until she came stumbling into the apartment yet again. Her eyes were swollen, her lip was cracked open, and there was blood on her chin. What had happened? To this day, I still don't know. She wouldn't tell me that night, and the next morning, she didn't remember.

Again, she begged for my forgiveness, and again, she received it. But the slipups became more frequent and more sporadic. Within a month, Sam lost her job. I swore up and down that I would leave her if she didn't pick herself up, but she begged me to stay. And I did exactly that.

"If you go, I'll never pick myself up. I don't have a job, Kaity!" she said.

Feeling that I was now responsible for her safety and well-being, I found I had fallen into a trap. Without me, she had no income. And without my income, she had no place to live. Why didn't I leave when the first warning signs appeared?

I wanted to help her—to save her. I realized how unhealthy that mentality was, but I didn't care. Eventually, Sam took a turn for the worse; her personality changed entirely, and she was no longer loving or nurturing in any sense of the word. She ignored me most of the time, and the only attention I ever received from her was in the form of accusations or demands for money.

September fourth was, I believe, the most devastating day of my life. I will never forget the date; not only did I have an interview to attend, it was also my sister's birthday party. These two things were both left unattended due to Sam.

It was Saturday morning when I woke to the sound of something collapsing in the bathroom. I sat up and listened attentively. Silence. There was a sudden drop in my stomach, and I knew something was wrong. I rushed to the bathroom and knocked loudly on the door.

"Sam?" I shouted.

Nothing. I reached for the handle—it was locked. I pounded on the door with my fists, but it was pointless.

"Sam?" I repeated.

So many thoughts rushed through my mind, and I feared the worst. With trembling hands, I dug my fingernail into the door handle's lock, twisted it, then burst the door open.

Sam was slouched up against the bathtub, a small needle in one hand and an elastic band strapped tightly around the elbow of her other arm. Her eyes were closed, and her jaw slack. Was she dead? My heart thudded hard against my ribs as I imagined attending her funeral. As adrenaline coursed through me, I rushed to her side and grabbed her face.

"Sam!" I shouted over and over and over again. I shook her hard and tore the needle from her hand.

Her head rolled back and forth, unresponsive.

"Sam!"

Suddenly, her green, sunken eyes rolled up at me, and she frowned.

"What?" she mumbled.

"Sam! What the fuck did you do?" I shouted. I was so afraid, so enraged, that I didn't know what to do with myself. I wanted to slap her hard, but at the same time, I wanted to pull her in and hold her, to let her know how much I loved her.

She moaned some incomprehensible sentence, and I shook her again.

"I'm calling 911." I jumped to my feet.

"Hey, wait," she moaned. She reached out and grabbed the bottom of my pants to hold me in place.

"You can't. Are you that stupid?" She leaned forward, her arms reaching for me.

"I have to," I said.

"Kaity..." She stretched herself out on the bathroom tiles. "Let me nap, I'm fine, baby," she said. "I'm fine, look. The tiles. I... I'm fine." She closed her eyes again.

Ignoring her, I walked out. There was no doubt in my mind that she needed an ambulance, and I wasn't going to sit around and let her overdose just because she was afraid of the law.

I went into the kitchen and pulled the phone from its receiver. My hands were still shaking, and I could feel my heart pounding against my ribs. I couldn't believe what was happening.

I had just enough time to hit the nine key, when Sam appeared behind me and tore the phone right out of my hands. Her mascara had leaked down one cheek, and her eyes were filled with so much ferocity that I wished I had dialed 911 for my own safety.

"Don't you listen?" she growled.

I stepped back a few feet, only to find myself pinned against the kitchen wall. I couldn't speak. I knew that no matter what I said, Sam wouldn't be the recipient. Was she even in there anymore? She scratched her head and stared at me for a second, her eyes hollow.

Her head rocked forward.

"Sam...?" I asked.

"Yeah, that's my name, don't wear it out," she slurred and walked away.

I couldn't believe it. How had I been so dense? How had I not seen this coming? I should have known there was more involved, more than alcohol, that is. Call me stupid, call me irrational, call me a nut job, call me crazy, call me a masochist, call me every damned word found in the unofficial dictionary of insults if you like; but no matter how many nasty remarks you throw my way, it still won't alter the fact that I stayed with Sam even after that awful day.

Knowing all too well that I was never going to receive the kind of love she had once given me, I realized I had no breaking point. Although I threatened to leave time and time again, I hadn't the strength in me to follow through. I knew she was better than what these substances made her out to be and that there was a beautiful person lost somewhere inside of her decaying body.

As the weeks went by, I began missing more days of work due to Sam's drug abuse. I feared the worst every day, knowing very well that I could leave work one day, only to come home to a corpse. Charlene allowed me to take a few weeks off but warned me that if I didn't return soon, they were going to have to hire someone else to replace me.

I didn't even know which drugs Sam was using. There were so many. There were pills, needles, powders. I hadn't the slightest clue how she was able to afford it all. I preferred to keep my head in the sand. All I did was wonder if she would ever come back to me. I hoped that my patience and understanding would make her realize that the world wasn't such a terrible place. I considered calling Maddi, but I didn't want to appear weak. I considered calling my parents but knew they wouldn't understand.

I accepted the torment for a few more weeks until finally, everything collapsed. She came home one evening digging through all sorts of papers and junk. Her frail, thin body was slouched over in the kitchen, and I could tell she was determined to find something specific.

"Fuck!" she shouted and threw some dishes on the floor.

The sound of glass shattering caused my shoulders to jerk forward, but there was nothing I could do to stop her. I didn't want to speak for fear of aggravating her. Her dark, colorless eyes shot up at me, and her eyebrows furrowed.

"You," she said.

I froze.

"Where'd you put it?" she asked, walking around the counter and into the living room.

"Put what?" I had no idea what she was referring to.

"The bus ticket! Don't play around, Kaity! They're coming here. I don't have time!" she shouted and scratched her greasy hair.

"I have no idea what you're talking about," I said.

"Liar!" she screamed, her face twisted in a demonic manner.

"Sam, I'm not lying. I swear."

I heard my own voice crack, and I knew I must have looked so pathetic curled up on the sofa. I noticed an odd smirk curve the corner of her lips, and she moved forward. I hesitated and backed away on the sofa. Her bony hand suddenly grabbed my leg, and I released a whimper. She was still smiling, and my heart was aching.

She slid her hand up my thigh and underneath my shirt. I suddenly realized that I was probably going to get raped by a girl. Her chapped lips kissed my jaw, my ears, and my neck. My entire body remained stiff. This wasn't love. This was manipulation at its worst. I closed my eyes and wished it away. Chills spread through my body, but I couldn't stop her. I was too afraid.

Her hand reached down into my pants, her cold fingers trying to tease me. I felt no desire, nor pleasure.

"Sam, please stop," I pleaded, my voice quivering.

"Stop? But you'll like it," she said and forced herself inside of me.

The feeling was awful, painful, even. I

squeezed my eyes shut and knew I would have to tough it out. Her movements became rough, and tears slid down my cheeks. I knew I could have pushed her off, hit her even. She was weak now, but I was still too afraid of her.

I didn't know what she would do to me if I reacted defensively. She finally tired herself out and dropped her head on my chest. I could feel my heart hammering against her cheek, but she didn't seem to realize how scared I was. She rested her hand on my chest, and I noticed a streak of blood soak into the material of my T-shirt. I quickly wiped my tears away.

"You coming?" she asked, suddenly looking up at me.

"Whe—" I cleared my throat. "Where?"

"I can't tell you right now. But if I stay here, they'll find me," she said.

"Who's they?" I asked.

"Shut up!" she hissed. "They can probably hear us now."

"Sam, are you joking?" I asked. But I knew this was a stupid question. She wasn't joking.

She sat up and glared at me, then jumped to her feet. "I'm not going to jail."

I watched as she disappeared into her bedroom and returned with her black school bag—the very same one she had been carrying the first day I met her. She was so different now. Her skin was almost transparent, her eyes had lost their glowing green, and her dark hair was oily and matted in different areas. Her beautiful, full figure had melted away and she was nothing more than a bag of bones.

"You coming or not?" she asked, slipping her shoes on.

"I can't," I said, my throat swelling.

I hoped that this psychotic break was temporary. I hoped she would be back within an hour or so. But I had no idea what she was doing or where she was going. Every time she left, I knew she may not return. And every time this routine occurred, the pain never failed to force tears from my eyes.

"Too bad. The sex was great." She swung the door open and walked out.

And whether or not she died that night, I can't even say for sure, because that was the last time I saw Samantha Boward.

Epilogue

"See you tomorrow," I said and hugged Bertram goodbye.

"You bet," he said, packing his bag.

I walked out of class and made my way to my car. The Lancer had been a gift from Andrew after he and my sister married. Looking back now, I can't believe how I had managed to survive without a vehicle. Sure, Loshano had a great bus system, but driving myself to any desired location was so much more practical.

I hopped in and drove to Amy and Andrew's place to pick up a book I had left there the week before.

"Hey, sis," Andrew said as I entered through the door.

He'd taken on the habit of referring to me as his sister immediately after their wedding. This, I assumed, was the result of not having any sisters himself. Although I'd had a little difficulty adapting at first, I thought it very cute that he considered me to be a part of his family. He was such a great guy, and I couldn't have been happier for Amy.

"Hey, Andrew. Where's preggo?" I asked, glancing around the kitchen wall.

"I told you to stop calling me that," Amy said, peering out from her bedroom.

Her stomach was enormous. One more month and she would be a mother. She and Andrew had already baby-proofed the entire house by putting little straps on the cabinet doors to keep them closed, by placing plastic covers on the sharp-cornered tables, and by getting rid of many unnecessary hazardous household items. I couldn't believe I was going to be an aunt to a baby girl. My parents, too, were so proud to be future grandparents.

"Here," she said, handing me one of my many Science textbooks.

I had left it there the previous weekend when my computer conveniently crashed the night before I was due to hand in a twenty-page essay. School was tough, but I was determined. I had one year left before beginning my career as a nurse, and I couldn't wait.

"Thanks," I said. "I'll see you guys soon, maybe supper at Mom and Dad's on Thursday?"

"Of course," Amy said, "I already asked Mom

to make that crazy vegetarian lasagna she used to make."

"Yum!" I said.

Her crazy vegetarian lasagna was the most mouthwatering meal anyone could ask for. We called it *crazy* since we had no idea what kind of vegetables she threw in there, but whatever they were, their deliciousness combined with melted cheddar and mozzarella cheese and tender pasta was to die for.

I waved them goodbye and jumped back into my car. I'm not sure what compelled me to do such a thing, but for old times' sake, I drove downtown to the same Subway Briana and I had gone to during my lunch break way back when. I was feeling somewhat reminiscent, and I just wanted a quiet meal to myself. I ordered my food and sat down at the far corner of the restaurant by the window. I could see the Loshano Inn from my seat, and I wondered if Charlene and Gloria were still working there. I wasn't going to go in to see, but the thought was there nonetheless.

I ate my food, remembering how Briana and I had shared such a pointless conversation here, and how she had invited me to Jacob's place for drinks that night. I wasn't big on partying anymore. I hadn't touched a drink after Sam left. What was the point? It was toxic, and I had experienced that toxicity firsthand.

I was now living in a bachelor's apartment on my own, going to school full-time, and working part-time at a local grocery store. The money wasn't great, but it was enough to pay rent, gas, and insurance for the time being. Maddi hadn't invited me to return to live with her, but she did offer to help me move and to help me in any other way possible. She was a sweetheart about the whole thing, but I understood that she also had herself to worry about. What if Sam did come back? Maddi surely wasn't going to be the one stuck in the middle of it all over again.

I sighed and finished my food. What if Sam did come back? I asked myself this question nearly every day since the day she left. I still missed her. Every night I went to bed, praying that she was safe wherever it was she had gone. I had a new phone number; I knew that allowing an open line of communication with Sam would only torture me further. I had to cut her out of my life entirely.

I grabbed my keys, thanked the guy behind the counter, and made my way outside. As I searched for my car, my eyes fell on something unexpected. I looked twice, three times, and four times to assure myself that I was registering what my eyes were seeing. I still couldn't believe it.

Right across the street, against the cold,

shiny wall of Loshano Bank, was Laura—Sam's friend. She was huddled up, her chin resting on her bony knees and her frail little arms wrapped around her legs. This couldn't be. She had been so sporty when I first met her, and now, it looked as though she would break if she tried to stand. Her eyes were swollen and dark underneath, her cheeks were sunken in, and her hair was so thin it looked as though she were balding.

My heart skipped a beat when her eyes slowly rolled my way. I didn't flee, nor did I try to pretend I hadn't seen her. Our eyes locked, and I knew she recognized me, regardless of how high or drunk she was.

Her face was so hopeless, so defeated. She didn't smile, or move, or try to stand. We stared at each other for what felt like minutes, and I became aware of the heartache Sam had brought into my life. I realized that for Laura, there was no going back. Seeing her this way brought forth an unwanted reality—Sam was no better than she was.

And for one selfish moment in time, I considered approaching Laura to ask her if she had seen Sam anywhere recently. I believe that not doing so is what saved me. I wanted to remember Sam as the beautiful, vibrant, green-eyed force who had so easily pulled me in and showed me what it was like to love someone.

She taught me the importance of choice, and the reality that we are who we choose to be, whether it leads to success or self-destruction. I had lost control of my own life once before; I would never again allow that to happen.

I finally turned away from Laura and entered my car. My fingers slid across the leather padding of my seats and gripped the steering wheel. I glanced at myself in the rearview mirror. I was healthy and in good physical shape. I had a family that loved me, my own apartment, and a future to look forward to.

But because I had focused all of my thoughts on Sam's life rather than my own, I never took the time to realize the truth that lay right before my eyes—I was in control of my life, and no person in the world would ever again have the power to take that away from me.

Visit **www.shadeowens.com** for more works by Shade Owens, including As I Fall – the prequel to Catch Me.

www.ingramcontent.com/pod-product-compliance
Lightning Source LLC
Chambersburg PA
CBHW030543190726
48283CB00006B/1995